TEARS OF THE GOD

JP WILDER

EDGE WEAVER BOOKS

Tears of the God

Edge Weaver Realms is an imprint of Edge Weaver LLC

Book Four of the Crusader Series

Book Design: Marie Pitrat

Kindle ISBN: 978-1-964406-18-3

Paperback ISBN: 978-1-964406-81-7

Edge Weaver LLC
19360 Rinaldi #681
Porter Ranch, CA 91326-1607

CONTENTS

Chapter 1
Hero's Return

I stood on the creaking deck of my barge, taking in the bustling riverside docks of Clurak. The briny tang of salt stung my eyes as I rubbed away the sleep.

The dockworkers, their bodies glistening with sweat under the relentless sun, moved with the urgency of a beehive. Crates and barrels were hoisted by pulleys, their creaking and groaning a symphony of labor. The crowds on the riverside docks were a chaotic chorus, voices haggling over prices, traders shouting out their wares, and the occasional clash of metal as a stubborn argument escalated.

Despite the smaller size of the docks compared to those facing the Sea of Sorrows, there was an undeniable energy in the air, a raw purpose amongst the longshoremen that brought back memories of when I first heard the Call to Crusade. Memories of battles fought, and lives lost. But that was long ago, and things were different. I was older, but perhaps no wiser. And the Crusade had become something of an enigma, a bitter war without purpose or direction. There were those who sought to give it one.

I shook the memories away. My body ached from the long journey, but my determination pushed me forward as I stretched, shook off the stiffness, and proceeded down the gangplank and into the throng.

Amongst the crowd, the sharp scent of sweat and the musty smell of fish permeated the air. The pungent odor of tar only added to the potent mixture, creating a familiar aroma that instantly flooded my mind with memories of this place. Memories I'd prefer to forget.

After five or six days on the River Rak, with only a tarpaulin for respite from the relentless sun, the stone and timber buildings of Clurak felt like a sanctuary. The hundred miles or more since

Caer Gorak had taken their toll on my body, but my mission was too urgent to delay any longer.

Anxiety gnawed at my gut as I approached the kingdom. The king's summons hung heavy over me, a weighty reminder of the gravity of my findings on the treacherous frontier. He knew I'd saved Ser Prenot Baudin against his dictum and my suspicions of the corrupt bishop. And most importantly, he knew of my thirst for retribution and justice for The God. Would he be waiting for me, ready to hear my plea? Or would he dismiss me as a traitor?

My musings ended abruptly when I heard my name called out. "My lord, Aaron!"

Ser Willem, my staunch and battle-tested captain, greeted me with a mix of relief and apprehension etched onto his weathered face. He grinned, his weathered face crinkling with mirth. "Well, well, if it isn't the great Aaron, Savior of the Realm, gracing us with his presence once more. I trust your journey was filled with tales of heroism and daring escapades?" His mirthful eyes, a vivid blue reminiscent of the harbor waters, sparkled with a mix of youthful spirit and resolve despite his years. Clad in a finely tailored tunic embla-zoned with our family's crest over his chain mail, the veteran soldier stood with an air of dignity and pride. As he neared, his face broke into a broad grin.

I couldn't help but chuckle, the weight of my troubles momentarily lifted by Willem's jovial tone. "If by heroism, you mean enduring endless days of stale biscuits and salt pork, then yes, I am a true hero."

I reached out and grasped his rough, cal-loused hand in mine. Despite years of crusad-ing—or perhaps because of it—his grip is firm and strong.

He placed a firm hand on my shoulder, relief clear in his eyes as he spoke. "I'm glad to see you unharmed," he said, his voice quiet but resolute. "We were worried that you would not come back. When we heard about . . ."

I waved him off, not wanting to think about the Lych who had become a frightening part of me. Edweene's presence lingered in my thoughts, her piercing blue eyes haunting my dreams and waking moments. I couldn't shake the memory of her feeding on Dumont, healing herself as she drained him, surrounded by an intoxicating darkness. And yet, a part of me longed to see her again, to feel that thrill in her presence. But at the same time, I couldn't help but fear what she might do next or if that blasted raven would appear again. It was a conflicting mix of hope and dread within me. It was a sacrilege against The God, that could cost me everything.

I met his gaze squarely and changed the subject back to the situation at hand. "The bishop's web of deceit has spread throughout this land. It's up to us to cut through it and return the Temple to the people of The God. Or this Crusade is a sham."

Ser Willem's brow furrowed in concern. "Be cautious; the bishop holds immense power within the king's court."

I narrowed my eyes, my gaze holding his. "I am aware of the risks, but some duties require sacrifice. I swore an oath when I took up the Call."

After a moment of contemplation, Willem gave me a nod of approval. "Wherever you lead, I will follow. And The God will protect us."

I wasn't so sure about the protection. I'd been doing a lot of fighting and killing for The God, and I rarely felt his hand guiding me or confounding my enemies. But perhaps that is the point. I was here now, in Clurack, doing The God's bidding—at least that was how I saw things. My enemies, however, were not so lucky. Perhaps that was evidence enough.

We exchanged a grim look as we squared our shoulders and turned towards the imposing keep. Our strides were confident, but my heart raced with trepidation. I'd have been portrayed as heroic and brave in days gone, and yet, I never felt it so. Today was no different. I put on the face of a brave knight, determined to serve the will of God, but my heart told a different story in its thundering staccato.

With each step, my breath grew shorter, and my knees trembled. We marched on, pretending to be confident and ready for whatever may come our way. But deep down, I was filled with uncertainty and fear. What if we were not as prepared as we thought? What if we couldn't handle the challenges that lay ahead? My mind was in turmoil, and I asked the God for comfort and made the sign of the Star on my chest.

We left the docks behind and entered the bustling streets of the Holy City. Despite my numerous visits during the Crusade, I could never get used to this place's overwhelming sights and sounds. The fortress in the distance towered over the city like a giant, its shadow looming over the peasantry, pilgrims, soldiers, and seamen. It was an awesome, foreboding place.

Ser Willem and I pushed through the crowded streets, unease wrapping around us like a fog. We caught hushed conversations and furtive glances from the townspeople, making me regret wearing my livery so openly. I pulled my traveling cloak closed.

Gazing upon the once-sacred walls of the Holy City, conflicting emotions weighed on me. Had the King strayed from righteousness because of the black-hearted bishop, or was it our collective corruption? My faith in the Crusade wavered; were we seeking vengeance instead of reformation? Doubts clouded my sense of purpose.

"I've a surprise," Willem's voice barely penetrated my thoughts as we continued the walk toward the central fortress.

Lost as I was contemplating the damage the bishop had caused, I scarcely recognized the figure that stepped out of the crowd to face me.

"Brother!" she cried.

The sound of my name being called startled me, but my surprise quickly faded as my sister enveloped me in a tight hug. Her arms wrapped around me like a warm blanket.

"Kira?" My voice cracked with emotion as I pulled her close, my arms enclosed her like a protective shield.

As she spoke, her voice trembling with relief and I felt her tears on my cheek. "When we heard about the ambush, I feared for your life. I've been waiting so anxiously for so long...I arrived weeks ago."

Guilt washed over me as I realized the worry and fear she must have been experiencing. "You should not have come," I murmured, but I couldn't help returned her embrace, grateful for her presence in the midst of chaos.

As I held Kira in my arms, all of it melted away. At that moment, her warmth against me and the sound of her breathing were the only things that mattered. My dark world, filled with anxiety, danger, and self-doubt, seemed to dissipate. The danger may still be present—even worse with her here in the Holy Land instead of back home—but I felt secure and calm in her embrace for a fleeting, foolish moment.

Kira's emerald eyes widened, the light catching on the flecks of gold in their depths. She instinctively pushed back a loose strand of her copper hair that had escaped from the intricate braid coiled around her head. Her delicate features twisted into a look of concern as she closely studied my expression. "Please, Aaron," she implored her voice tight with worry. "Tell me the truth. Is it truly as dire as Ser Willem suggests?" I hesitated, not wanting to weigh her down with the full weight of political schemes and violence that plagued our kingdom.

But Kira was always perceptive; she would see through any false reassurances. With a heavy sigh, I nodded. "The bishop plans to break the truce . . . or rather, to incite the Gols to break it. And I fear he has succeeded. The Crusade is becoming restless camped around this city. It is starting to crumble from within. Knights and lords are taking their armies home—he intends to give them a purpose, a reason to stay. This goes against the will of The God and even the Archbishop himself. And it is all being done in secrecy; dark forces are at work here."

Ser Willem's brow furrowed with concern as he stepped closer to me, his hand gripping the hilt of his sword. "It's true," he confirmed, his voice low and urgent. "Even our most seasoned sergeants and soldiers are growing restless and angry. They came here for a Crusade, but instead, they are stuck in this city, bored and plagued by sickness. Their frustration is turning towards innocent people, both among the Heathen and within our own walls. It's becoming increasingly difficult to keep them under control; even the holy knights and priests are lashing out at those who don't deserve it."

I paused, considering my next words carefully before speaking. "Better that than . . ." I started to said.

But Ser Willem cut me off with a sharp shake of his head. "My Lord, let us not speak such blasphemy. Dying on the Crusade may be difficult, but it is also the highest honor one can achieve. To die of a disease, wasting away in a tent is seen as cowardice by the Temple. I understand your point, but please do not mention it again."

I took a deep breath, feeling the weight of my responsibility heavily upon my shoulders. "Honor," I said slowly, "is not just about who we kill or how we die. The Crusade was once necessary to protect our people from massacre at the hands of the Heathen. But now . . . things have changed."

My words trailed off as I looked at Kira, seeing the worry in her eyes. Ser Willem continued, his tone serious and earnest. "With due respect, my lord, Lady Kira is right to be concerned. This situation with the bishop does not feel right. There may be more danger here in this city than on any battlefield."

I met their gazes, moved by their loyalty and concern for me. But I could not turn away from this path. "I understand the risk," I said firmly. "But I made an oath to uncover the truth. If the bishop is acting against the archbishop and the will of The God, he must be stopped."

Kira searched my face, clearly dismayed by my decision. But she could also see the determination in my eyes, and she knew that I would not back down from this mission. At last, she nodded. "Then we will help you see this through."

I gripped her shoulder, taking comfort in her unwavering faith. With Kira and Ser Willem flanking me, we navigated through the winding streets of Clurak. The city was strangely subdued the further up the mount we went. The usually bustling crowds now muted and watchful. Gone was the lively chaos I remembered from just a few years past. It was never a joyous place, forged as it was in warfare and the strict dictums of the King and the bishop of Tears, who resided in Clurak's imposing Temple of Tears. But it was united in The Crusade and in its defense of the Holy Land. Now, the people avoided eye contact and clung to the shadows, as if afraid to draw any attention.

A feeling of unease clawed at my insides, making every step up the hill feel heavier. This place had changed since I was last here, and not for the better. The stone walls of the central structure were worn and aged, bearing the marks of time and conflict. High above, the royal banner flapped in defiance against the winds. As we neared the gates, I could see the king's men stationed there stiffen, their weapons ready but cautious. They relaxed slightly as they recognized me, but their wary eyes still followed our every move.

"Ser Aaron," their sergeant greeted with a respectful bow of his head. "We've been expecting you."

The gate sergeant gave a sharp nod, and the iron gates slowly creaked open. We were met inside by a knight wearing the king's livery. He bowed slightly to us, and we returned the courtesy. Without a word, he turned on his heel and led us in. He kept a firm grip on his sword's hilt, and his keen gaze darted this way and that. Was his posture for us or other would-be intruders? My paranoia was getting the best of me. And I began to see phantoms in every shadow—not so different than on campaign. Somewhere, somehow, this war had turned me into a man who saw threats everywhere.

The fortress was eerily quiet as we made our way deeper into its heart. We passed through an open hall and a ladies' sitting room that looked out over the glittering Sea of Sorrows. The king's man slowed not at all until, at last, he led us down a long hallway lined with doors on either side. I couldn't help but feel we were being watched, and the hairs on my neck stood on end.

Ser Willem leaned in close to me, his voice barely a whisper. "Do you think we are in danger here?" I shook my head, not wanting to alarm Kira, who walked ahead. "No, I believe they are just being cautious." Willem nodded, but I could see the tension in his stance as he kept a firm grasp on his pommel.

As we made our way down the hallway, the Knight stopped before two oaken doors. The dim light of oil lamps, suspended from iron shackles above, cast shadows across the intricate carvings on the door. "In here, your grace," announced the sergeant with a low bow. "Your private chambers have been prepared for you." He turned to my sister and added, "And yours as well, my lady."

Kira gave a small nod of gratitude as she stepped into her room. I followed suit and thanked the knight before he took his leave. I couldn't help but notice the visible relief in his posture as he made his exit. With a heavy thud, the doors closed behind him.

I took a moment to survey my new surroundings, taking note of the arrow slits that overlooked the bustling city below. The chamber was sparsely furnished but exuded an aura of security and protection that I would not indulge in.

Before I could turn to speak to Kira and Willem, something on the bed caught my eye: a folded parchment with a familiar crimson seal lay atop the sheets. Without hesitation, I crossed over and broke the seal, revealing the unmistakable mark of Gavreaux.

CHAPTER 2
SHADOWS OF DOUBT

The wax seal cracked under the force of my thumb. Behind me, I heard our door open and Kira's voice. She and Willem were discussing something inconsequential. I ignored it and unfolded the parchment. As I read Ser Gavreaux's carefully written words, I could feel their literal and symbolic weight pressing down on me. His script danced with a formality that belied the urgency of his message, every stroke of ink a silent herald of the dangerous game we were now to play.

Ser Aaron—

Under the shadow of the crescent moon, our fates converge. Seek out Ser Renart at the Wounded Boar, where mead drowns sorrows and secrets are traded like coin. Trust in what he offers; it is time to unveil the bishop's grand design.

The letter bore only that, yet it spoke volumes. The Knight Commander risked much in seeking my alliance. Clurak was the domain of Ser Transom, Commander of the Knights of Tears, not his Passage knights. The two orders did not like one another, each vying for the ear of the bishop—and the archbishop. But it was a beacon in the night to me, from a powerful man, giving me hope and admonishing me to beware the accompanying peril.

I let the silence of the chambers envelop me once again. The parchment crackled softly as I refolded it. Deliberation clawed at my thoughts. How often had I found myself ensnared in webs woven of deceit and ambition? And yet, Gavreaux's call was a clarion I could not ignore, which promised answers to the labyrinthine treachery that threatened to strangle the very crusade I had bled for.

The looming darkness of the tent city skulked beyond my window, a sprawling expanse of canvas and desperation where the Wounded Boar lay somewhere out there—hidden like a secret sin. Renart, a knight with a tarnished reputation, awaited there amid the ale-soaked squalor.

My hand instinctively reached for the hilt of my sword, resting against the rough-hewn table. The steel whispered reassurances of protection and resolve, but it could not shield me from the uncertainty that now coursed through my veins like a chill wind. Would this clandestine meeting light the path to redemption or lead me further into a mire of falsehoods?

"Steel yourself, Aaron," I muttered under my breath. Resolve hardened within me, a fortress built upon the bedrock of duty and a thirst for truth. Tonight, I would meet with Renart, cloaked in the secrecy of Gavreaux's bidding. Tonight, I would either unearth the seeds of betrayal sown deep within the heart of our holy endeavor, or I would find myself ensnared in a trap of my own making.

And so, with the dying embers of twilight as my witness, I readied myself for the inevitable confrontation that loomed before me, as daunting and uncertain as the war that raged just beyond the reach of the King's tenuous grasp.

"Kira, Willem," I called my voice a hushed command that sliced through the murmurs of our hidden chamber. As they approached, I passed the letter to them, a silent testament of trust amongst us.

"By the God," Kira breathed, her usual composure giving way to awe. "The Knight Commander himself . . ." She looked up, eyes alight with the fire of hope. "Aaron, this could be our chance! Our cause has found favor in powerful eyes."

Willem, ever the bastion of skepticism, took the letter with a scowl etched deep into his weathered face. "Renart," he grunted as if the name were a curse. "His honor is questionable at best. I've seen men like him—knights in naught but a title, serpents slithering through the grasses of our nobility."

"Yet we must seize this opportunity, must we not?" I argued, my conviction steeling against his doubt. "If Renart holds the key to the bishop's schemes, then we are bound by duty to pursue it."

Willem's gaze met mine, an unspoken challenge lingering in the air between us. "Aye," he conceded, "but keep your hand close to your sword, Ser Aaron. Trust is a luxury ill-afforded on such a night."

Their words, one a beacon of faith, the other a shroud of caution, swirled within me. Thorns bordered the path I walked, each step a potential descent into betrayal. "Prepare yourselves," I instructed, my resolve a cloak wrapped tight around my shoulders. "Tonight, we dance with shadows."

I slipped the letter from Gavreaux into my tunic, letting his words sink in. They were like a discordant symphony playing in my mind. My heart raced with worry, not just about the dangers of navigating these political games but also because of Edweene's warnings back at Caer Gorak, which still haunted me.

"Trust him not, Aaron," her voice echoed through the veil of memory, as ethereal and chilling as the ghostly winds that whisper across Gol's forsaken barrens. "Gavreaux is a zealot—a blade seeking redemption, with little care for the cost, whether it is borne by heretic or innocent." She loathed the man who had abandoned her, even as he lifted me from the mire of my reckoning.

I could almost feel her icy hand on my arm as if she were still there. Her menacing features and unnerving azure eyes made her a haunting presence. Her hatred for the Knight Commander was only matched by our strange, intense connection.

As the sun set, a raven's call broke through the silence of the dusk. I searched for its source but could only see shadows growing longer as night approached. Could be the castle's rookery. But I felt different. It was her sign, watching me from afar. It was always her sign. A pang of guilt twisted within my breast at the thought of the clandestine meeting I pursued, for how could I align with the one whom Edweene vowed to destroy?

"Ser Aaron," Willem's gruff voice drew me back to the present, his silhouette framed against the flickering torchlight. "It's time we depart."

"Indeed," I murmured, steeling myself against the fears that threatened to unseat my purpose. With a last glance toward the heavens, seeking the silent observer I knew lurked just beyond sight, I followed Willem and the knight into the corridor.

"Willem," I said, voice low, as the torches sputtered in the drafty chamber. "Renart awaits us at the edge of civility and chaos. We must tread carefully, but we cannot delay."

Willem's eyes narrowed, his scarred visage betraying a roiling sea of skepticism beneath his stoic exterior. "I'll ride with you into the abyss, Aaron. But mark my words, Renart is no steadfast guide."

A nod was all I could muster in gratitude. Any sentiment beyond that felt frivolous, a luxury unbefitting the gravity of our path.

Before we could depart, the door burst open, admitting an unseasonable chill and the King's man, his cloak billowing like the standard of impending doom.

"Ser Aaron, the King summons you," he said, his voice devoid of the customary reverence one might expect when addressing a knight of the realm.

Kira glanced at me with veiled concern, her eyes reflecting a tumult of unvoiced fears. Our garb was far from courtly—we had not had time, as we were promised, to bathe or even change our travel-stained clothing. The knight waved off our wordless apologies.

"His Majesty cares little for the sheen of silk nor the pomp of courtiers," he declared.

"Then we shall attend him, as we are" I replied, my heart leaden with foreboding yet buoyant with resolve.

We strode confidently through the winding passageways of the stronghold, the resounding thud of our footsteps a lament for the tranquility we had abandoned. The presence of my sword at my hip was a soothing reassurance, a determined promise to protect justice against the encroaching darkness that loomed nearer.

"Remember, Aaron," Kira whispered as we approached the threshold of the king's presence. Words are oft sharper than blades in the halls of power. Wield them wisely."

As the heavy doors swung open, revealing the audience chamber, I prepared myself for the confrontation to come. As I entered the chamber, I caught sight of a short and robust, balding man in temple robes slipping out through a side door. It was Maester Aldric, one of the bishop's most trusted advisors. I knew him from my time with the Dark Men. He often oversaw our singularly dark missions. He paused for a moment, his cold eyes meeting mine, and a sneer curled his thin lips.

"Ser Aaron," he said, his voice dripping with disdain. "I see you've returned from your misadventures on the frontier. How fortunate for you that the King sees fit to grant you an audience despite the chaos you've sown."

Before I could respond, Aldric turned on his heel and disappeared through the doorway, his robes swirling behind him. The exchange left a bitter taste in my mouth, and I couldn't shake the feeling that the Maester's presence here boded ill for our cause.

The chamber was not the gilded hall of audiences but a dimly lit antechamber, heavy with the

scent of beeswax and a somber air of contemplation. The king's silhouette loomed ahead, framed
by the flickering hearth. I hesitated, unsure what
to do. The knight bowed to the king's back and
slipped back out the door, closing it with a thud.

"Ser Aaron," His Majesty intoned, his voice devoid of warmth as he regarded us across the expanse of shadows that danced between us. "Your
valor in returning Prenot Baudin to the fold is
noted. The Earless is Monae Baoudin is pleased
with his return, no doubt. Except, as fate would
have it, they lost another."

I bowed, my armor creaking with the motion—a
resonant accompaniment to the gravity of the
moment. "My liege, it was my sworn duty. And
Dumont was . . ."

The sharp jab of Willem's elbow in the ribs
caught me up short. "Enough, Aaron." The voice,
scarcely louder than a whisper, cut through the
tension like a well-honed dagger. Willem's hand
had found its way to my arm, a subtle clamp of
warning.

I turned slightly to regard him, my trusted companion, and in his eyes, I saw reason. His head

gave the faintest of shakes, and I knew his counsel was sound. Do not speak accusations without proof, lest you trade your neck for your pride.

"Forgive me, Sire," I said, reigning in the tempest of my accusations. "The strain of recent events has frayed the edges of my composure."

"Indeed," the king replied, steepling his fingers, eyes glinting like shards of ice in the firelight. "Yet yours was a venture fraught with peril, one I expressly forbade. Had you faltered, the executioner would have claimed another soul—or perhaps the breaking star would have found some use."

A shiver coursed down my spine at the mention of that torturous device, its name alone conjuring images of unspeakable pain. I thought of the man I'd found on that perilous trek to Deveaux's estate, broken and dead upon the star. A warning to me, it had been, to stop my journey. And now, I hear of it again.

"Ser Dumont's absence weighs heavily upon us," the king continued, his words slicing through the hush. "A valiant knight, irreplaceable in this precipice of war."

"His sacrifice will be honored," I said, my throat tight as if the noose had already encircled it. The king nodded, though his gaze held a calculation that sent a tremor through me.

"Your deeds have placed me upon the horns of a dilemma, Ser Aaron," he declared with a measured cadence. "To chastise you would sow discord among the crusaders; to laud you stokes flames that may consume us all."

"Your wisdom in these troubled times shall guide us, colored as they are with the wisdom of The God," I offered, each word laced with bitterness. "I am ever your loyal servant, bound by blood and honor."

"Let us hope that honor does not lead us down a path from which there is no return." The king's eyes narrowed, and in their depths, I saw the reflection of every sin I had ever committed in the name of the Holy Crusade. His lips parted to unleash another torrent upon me . . . but it was Kira who stopped it with the grace only she possesses.

She spoke softly, her voice calming the tense air. "Ser Aaron is loyal to the realm and the Will of The God, his actions showing his devotion. His bravery in the face of darkness gives hope in these troubled times. And your grace's courage in allowing him his faults speaks to wisdom and mercy, both pillars of The God's teachings." Her smile was charming, disarming even the most guarded. With confidence in her words, she complimented both me and the king.

The king eventually nodded, his tension easing slightly. Her words relieved the pressure in the room, a sign of her intellect and beauty. "It's settled then," the king said sternly. "But remember, Ser Aaron: we are walking on a thin line between chaos and order."

"With your permission, Your Majesty." I bowed before leaving with her and Ser Willem. The shadows of the chamber hinted at dangers outside our safe walls as our footsteps echoed like a warning for what was to come.

CHAPTER 3
WHISPERS IN THE DARK

W e hurriedly exited the audience chamber, the weighty doors slamming shut behind us, echoing throughout the hall. As soon as we were far enough away that no one could hear us, I leaned in close to him.

"Willem, we depart for the camp at once," I whispered, urgency lacing my words.

The corridors of the castle were dim, lit by flickering torches that cast long shadows on the stone walls. They seemed to reach for us, as if the very darkness itself was alive, whispering secrets of treachery and deceit. I could feel eyes upon us, unseen watchers noting our every move.

"Ser Aaron, brother," Kira's voice broke through my thoughts, carrying a weight of sorrow. "I am staying."

Her gaze lingered on mine, a silent storm of emotions brewing in her eyes. Understanding passed between us, an unspoken bond. But her staying was dangerous, unprotected, alone. "Kira, I need you to come with us," I said, my tone brooking no argument. "The castle is not safe, not with the bishop's men potentially lurking in every shadow."

She met my gaze, her eyes flashing with determination. "Aaron, I can do more good here than out there. I have friends in the court, people who trust me and confide in me. If there's a plot afoot, I'll hear whispers of it."

I opened my mouth to protest, but she held up a hand. "I know you worry, brother, but I am not a helpless maiden. I can take care of myself."

And what could I say? Her statement was correct. She'd managed the household in my absence. Mustered the men, appointed Willem, and sent him to Crusade. All while I chased the lych and my demons. She was strong. As strong as I, perhaps stronger. I nodded. "Be careful," I managed to say over the lump in my throat.

"Always," she replied. She hesitated for more than a moment. I meant to leave, when at last she continued. "Aaron, I know the path you tread is dangerous," Kira said, her voice softening. "But remember, you don't have to face this alone. I'm here for you, not just as your sister, but as someone who believes in your cause."

I placed a hand on her shoulder, a gesture of reassurance and gratitude. "I know, Kira. Your support means more than you can imagine. But I need you to stay safe. The enemies we face are ruthless and will stop at nothing to maintain their grip on power."

Kira met my gaze, her eyes shining with determination. "I understand. But don't underestimate me, brother. I have my own ways of fighting for what's right. I'll be your eyes and ears within the palace, gathering what information I can to aid your cause."

I couldn't help myself. I leaned over and pulled her in. "I do love you sister, and would never underestimate you. Thank you."

She smiled and pulled away. "Get you gone," she said and hurried away.

As Willem and I made our way out of the castle, the evening air greeted us with a chill that penetrated to the bone. We hastened our pace, crossing the courtyard toward the stables where our steeds awaited, their breaths clouding in the cool night.

"Ser Aaron," Willem said, his voice still tinged with concern, "are you certain about this? Renart is a shadowy figure, and we tread on dangerous ground. Though I must say, it makes for interesting bedfellows. Having you here fills me with joy, my lord," he laughed.

And I laughed at his mirth but spoke to the seriousness in his question, "Certainty is for kings, not for knights like us," I said, my resolve hardening. "We must act, or we'll just be puppets in someone else's game."

As we mounted our horses, the clatter of hooves against the cobblestone echoed like the distant rumble of thunder. I led the way, my mind racing with thoughts of Renart and the

King—both enigmas in a world where truth was an elusive thing.

"Keep a watchful eye," I instructed, my voice barely above a whisper. "There are forces at play here that would sooner see us dead than victorious."

"By The God, ser, I thought I'd relax and sleep walk through this," he mocked me.

I shook my head and grinned back at him. It was nice to have someone so carefree with me, although I believed he intended his jokes to alleviate his own nervousness as much as mine.

Without another word, we rode out from the sanctuary of the castle into the night, the darkness enveloping us like a cloak. It was a descent into uncertainty, I don't mind saying. I was not sure what awaited us.

The chill of the night seeped into my bones as Willem and I hastened through labyrinthine streets. As we approached the yawning gate marking the end of the city's embrace, a figure detached itself from the darkness to our flank from within a nearby alleyway, its movements serpentine and fluid.

My years with the Dark Men had taught me about shadows and stealth. I knew an unnatural darkness when I saw it. Other men may have been fooled, but I immediately knew that this murderer was targeting us.

"Ser Willem" I said, "to your left!" My warning pierced the quietude, and I spun in my stirrup, my blade unsheathed in a whisper of steel against leather.

The Gol's curved dagger gleamed with lethal promise, aimed for his heart. But Willem was not yet ready to yield his spirit to The God. Parrying the strike, he countered with a swift thrust that slid along the man's shoulder, opening a gash and spraying blood over the cobbles.

It was bloody, but shallow, and the assassin danced back. "Death comes, knights," the Gol hissed, his words slithering through the darkness like a venomous adder. "Your blood will appease the shadows."

As I spurred my horse towards him, I retorted, "Let them be sated with yours," and leaned into a slash aimed to crash through his parry. And it almost did. The heavy blade collided with his dagger, forcing his arm to collapse downward, but he skillfully spun out from under the slash and swiftly moved away, while my momentum propelled me forward. With a burst of adrenaline, I spun my horse around, ready for another powerful strike.

"Enough playing! Kill the bastard!" Willem spurred his animal into the fray, his broadsword slicing through the night air. The Gol responded to his cry by swiftly redirecting its attention away from me and successfully parrying another potentially fatal blow. But then, I saw my moment. With a swift motion, I plunged my sword deep into the Gol's side, sliding it under his raised arm. He let out a guttural scream, the sound echoing through the air as he stumbled, leaving a trail of crimson lifeblood on the cobblestones.

"Finish it," Willem growled, his blade gleaming in the dim light, ready to strike the final blow.

I met the Gol's gaze, his eyes wide with the realization of his fate. "May your gods find you worthy," I whispered before driving my sword through his chest, granting him release from his mortal coil.

Willem leaped from his mount, rushed to the dying assassin, and slit his throat. Finished, he wiped his blade clean on the assassin's tunic, a wry grin on his lips. "Well, that's one way to make new friends in this city. Think he'll invite us for a drink next time?"

I couldn't help but chuckle, the tension in my chest easing slightly. "I doubt it, Willem. But if he does, let's hope the ale is better than the company."

We stood there for a moment, the echo of battle ringing in our ears, before dragging the corpse into the shadows, concealing it beneath a pile of refuse. Our cries likely alerted someone, and the last thing we needed was an incident to spark hostilities amidst an already teetering truce.

"Let us away," I said, sheathing my sword with a shiver that had naught to do with the cold. "Renart awaits, and with him, perhaps, the key to unraveling this web of treachery." The shadow of the assassin fell over my mind. Another dead in this war—a stark reminder of mortality amidst the chaos that had erupted around us.

We moved quickly, navigating through tents and shanties, dodging Crusaders and camp followers alike. The camp was alive with the voices of men and the clangor of smiths, wagons, horses and all the sounds that came with a military camp—it all magnified the trepidation we had about our destination and the shadow figure we were to meet.

Soon, we reached the edge of the camp, leaving the lion's share of its discord behind. The sounds of the bivouac faded as we approached the makeshift inn. It stood forlornly against the backdrop of a starless sky, its structure a haphazard assembly of wood and canvas destined to be deconstructed or left to decay once the crusade marched onward.

Inside, the air was thick with the scent of spilled ale and the raucous laughter of men who sought to forget the war or combat the boredom that came with soldiering. We found our table, cloaked in darkness far from the meager fire pit, that belched smoke through a crude hole that served as a chimney.

A strange silence settled between us. Willem was a comfortable companion, and one with whom I felt no need to converse about shallow things.

Still, I spoke to reassure myself. "Renart will come," I murmured, more to convince myself than Willem. Our meeting with the knight could well tilt the scales of this clandestine war in which we found ourselves entangled.

"Let him," Willem grunted, his distrust a palpable thing. "And let him bring answers that shine light upon these shadows."

I made to answer, as a smile slid across his face. He raised his tankard. "If he doesn't, we'll still get drunk. And you need a good drunk. Boy do you."

I smiled at him and swallowed my answer. We waited, the minutes stretching into eternity. And then, as if summoned by our impatience, a figure emerged from the crowd. Shrouded in a dark cloak, hood pulled up, and took his seat across from us, the shadows seeming to cling to him.

"Renart, I presume," I said. A statement, not a question.

"Ser Aaron," he intoned, his voice low and resonant. "I had hoped for a private audience, but it seems your . . . associate has other ideas."

Willem bristled, his hand inching toward the hilt of his sword.

"Peace, Willem," I said, my hand staying his. "Let us hear what the knight has to say."

Even as I leaned forward to listen, a raven perched on the windowsill captivated my attention, its piercing blue eyes staring at me with uncanny intelligence. Instinctively, I nodded to the creature, causing Willem to raise an eyebrow in confusion. As it cocked its head, I could almost hear it say, "I understand, I'm here for you."

My attention back, I spoke to our would-be conspirator. "Ser Renart," I began, my voice hesitant and laced with caution, the words weighed down with apprehension. "Your message was cryptic. What peril beckons that we must convene in this somber corner of night?"

"Peril is the cloak all men wear here, Ser Aaron," he replied, his voice a low hum that seemed to resonate with the very stones of the ramshackle inn.

"Indeed," Willem jocked. "Let's dispense with the mad theatrics, spy, and talk openly, if quietly."

A pause hung in the air, as Renart considered my companion. "I've been waiting for you. Though again, perhaps you shall send away your lackey."

Willem bristled at the remark, eyes narrowing into slits.

"Willem has proven his mettle repeatedly," I countered, my own hand steadying Willem's with a firm grip. "He is no mere lackey, but a trusted comrade-in-arms."

"Ah, loyalty," Renart mused, a sardonic twist to his lips. "A noble sentiment. But it can be . . . blinding." His gaze flitted between us.

"Speak plainly, Ser Renart," I pressed, leaning closer.

"I suppose you are right. Time for pleasantries has long since passed," Renart whispered, his eyes glinting with an intensity. "The bishop's pawns march to a sinister tune, one that could jeopardize your standing, and, far worse, the Crusade itself."

"Then let us be swift to act," I declared, though doubt gnawed at the edges of my conviction. This meeting was a gambit, and I had yet to discern whether Renart was ally or another piece on the enemy's board. "Now, what are your words, man? What do you know?"

Renart leaned forward, his voice dropping to a whisper. "The bishop's ambition knows no bounds. He intends to strike at the very heart of the Crusade—to kill the King himself and lay the blame at the feet of the Gols. With the King dead and the kingdom in chaos, the bishop plans to place Knight Commander of the Temple Knights at the head of the Crusade, seize control of the army, and lead the charge against our enemies."

I felt my blood run cold at his words. The thought of the bishop orchestrating such a heinous act was almost too much to comprehend. "If he succeeds," Renart continued, "the war that your rescue of the young knight nearly started will erupt in full force, with the bishop's man at the head of the host and the Archbishop unable to speak against it. The consequences would be catastrophic, not just for the Crusade, but for the entire Kingdom of The God."

I exchanged a glance with Willem, the weight of Renart's revelation hanging heavy between us. "How do we stop him?" I asked, my voice tight with determination. "What proof do you have of this treachery?"

Renart's eyes glinted in the flickering light, a hint of a smile playing at the corners of his mouth. "There are those that know. Look for the word to come to you at your tent."

"When man?" I came to you tonight, looking for information that I could—"

"Patience, ser," he said. "Patience—it is one of The God's virtues, is it not? Word will come. I promise you. In what form, I don't yet know." With that dismissal, he rose from the table, his cloak swirling around him like a shroud of secrets. As he melted into the shadows, I felt the burden of our mission settling upon my shoulders.

As we pondered the gravity of Renart's words, a thought occurred to me. "What of Knight Commander Transom?" I asked, my brow furrowed.

"The Knights of Tears are sworn to protect the Holy City and the Temple. If the bishop's plan succeeds, Transom stands to gain a great deal of power."

Willem nodded, his expression grim. "Aye, and Transom is known for his unwavering loyalty to the Temple. If the bishop has promised him a place at the head of the Crusade, he may well be involved in this plot."

"If the plot is true at all." I sighed, the weight of our task growing heavier by the moment. "We must tread carefully, Willem. We do not even know this is real. You yourself have questioned this madman. And his demeanor gives me no comfort that it is true. Transom's influence runs deep; if he is in league with the bishop, he will stop at nothing to see this plan through."

CHAPTER 4
SECRETS AND BETRAYALS

The flickering candlelight cast an eerie glow in my command tent as Willem and I pored over Gavreaux's parchment, its cryptic words taunting us with their hidden meaning. We'd returned to our quarters after the unsettling meeting with Renart, our minds heavy with the weight of his revelations. After a quick nap, we'd awakened in order to plan a course of action. "*Under the Shadow of the Crescent Moon* . . . what does that mean?" I asked rhetorically.

Opting for his customary approach, Willem quipped, "I reckon the old goat is just trying to sound all mysterious and whatnot."

I looked out the flap of a window on the tent and scoffed at his joke. It seemed unlikely that the Knight Commander would do something merely to flourish. And, like a fool, I'd forgotten to ask Renart about it. The moon was nearly crescent now and waning. It would not be long—a night or two—what could it mean? Is this murder to take place then, or is something else to happen? Or was it something else entirely? A symbol? No answers came to me.

In a low voice, I muttered the perilous words Renart had said, "The bishop's ambition knows no bounds." While I spoke, my fingers delicately traced the elaborate patterns of the Gavreaux's inked lines. Were the two connected in any way? His ambition and this crescent moon? I looked at Willem, who stared back, concern in his eyes. I said, "If what Renart says is true, we're not just fighting for the Crusade anymore. We're fighting for the soul of the kingdom."

Willem nodded grimly, his brow furrowed. "Aye, and with Transom potentially involved, we're up against a formidable foe. The man's loyalty to the Temple is unshakable."

I sighed, leaning back in my chair. "We must find what is meant by crescent moon. If it is a clock, we are already nearly out of time."

"I had not thought it thus," Willem said. "But you are right. When we meet Renart's man—"

"Or lady," I corrected.

"Or lady, we must press it from him . . . or her."

"I agree," I said. I went back to my pondering. All this was confounding. And the raven's presence at the inn haunted me too; its piercing blue eyes reminded me of all my mistakes and sins against The God: Edweene—she was, at once, my greatest achievement and my greatest failure. "And what of the Edweene?" I asked. I thought I was speaking to myself, but I was thinking aloud, like a fool. "Her reach seems to extend further than we thought."

Willem shrugged, his expression guarded. "I don't know this Edweene, my lord. But, from the volumes you speak of her, she most be lovely beyond measure—and have the heart of Nun." He laughed out loud at his own joke, as he often does.

Nun—the mention of the Wives of the God, sent my heart to pounding. Edweene was indeed a Wife of the God on pilgrimage when the heathen had taken her. What they'd done to her—I shook the thought away and choked back those horrible memories.

Not knowing of my anguish, Willem continued, his voice full of delight. "Though you talk of her often. Even in your sleep . . ." At last, he pulled up short when he saw the grimace on my face. "Best not to dwell on it, Aaron," he said, serious now. "We've got bigger problems to worry about."

He was right, but I couldn't shake the feeling that Edweene's involvement would complicate matters even further. And I could not get those eyes out of my head. I did my best to push the thought aside and focus on the task ahead of me. I said to Willem, "Renart said the word would come to us. We need to be ready when it does."

A scratching on the canvas sounded at the tent flap as if on cue. Willem and I exchanged a glance, hands instinctively reaching for our weapons. I rose, approaching the portal cautiously. "Who goes there?"

"A message for Ser Aaron," a muffled voice replied.

I opened the door, revealing a sergeant in my livery. I recognized him at once as Deres of Faulk, a competent soldier and one of my men, which relieved me greatly, given the day's events. He handed me a parchment and nodded. "Given me by a hooded man, ser," he said. "I did not get his name before he disappeared."

"Thank you, Deres," I said. I nodded back.

The sergeant took a step back, then melted into the shadows. I unfolded the note, my heart pounding as I read the words scrawled in a hasty hand.

"The truth lies beneath the Weeping Stone, beneath the forgotten fall. Seek the sightless one."

Willem peered over my shoulder, "Another riddle? Renart certainly enjoys his games."

I shook my head, a spark of understanding igniting in my mind. "Not a game. A clue. The Weeping Stone . . . I've heard whispers of a place in the lower city, a dark place, mocking of The God. And . . . I am told a place of shadowy enterprise."

Willem's eyes widened. "You think that's where we'll find our answers?"

"It's a start," I said, pocketing the note. "We leave at first light. The sightless one must be our informant."

Sleep eluded me that night, my thoughts consumed by the challenges that lay ahead. As dawn broke, Willem and I set out into the city, cloaks pulled tight against the morning chill. The streets were quiet, the only sound the echo of our footsteps on the cobblestones.

We wove through narrow alleys and darkened corners. The Weeping Stone was a place that most men of quality would avoid. Named, in mockery, of the place where The God was sacrificed for us, it held all the auspicious promise the name implied. It was not a place for noblemen or knights. We left our livery behind, though we would not forgo our steel. We draped plain smocks over our chain hauberks and strapped plain swords to our hips.

I'd known of the place as a Dark Man. Our profession sometimes took us to such places as we hunted the spies of the Heathen. I knew just where it was. Memories of those days slid, like serpents, through my mind as we slipped through the darkened alleyways of the Holy City's more unwelcoming parts—the parts no one back in Bannnonshire knew of because admitting it would be to admit the failures of the bishop and his Holy Decrees.

It was not long before the air grew thick with the stench of human excrement and unwashed bodies as we descended into the bowels of the city. I led Willem down an unnamed alleyway. Above us, lines ran between ramshackle clay and rotten-wood structures, and the tattered clothing of the slave and peasant class hung for drying after being scrubbed or shaken by the ghosts of people who lived within. The alleyway stunk of refuse poured and dumped from the windows above.

"A nice place," Willem said. "Your former haunts are worrying to me, my lord," he quipped.

"The best place for finding killers and spies," I said. "And only slightly more honest than those in the Temple of Tears and the halls of the palace." I joked back.

"Touche, ser," he said.

At last, the weathered statue came into view—a broken man, carrying a great, six-pointed star, set in a circular wheel-like device, bent at the waist and covered in scars, stumbling over a stone. Stone tears rolled down the tortured man's cheeks. It was the effigy of The God. He hid in an alcove, His eyes fixed on the stone in the ground in an eternal lament. I approached cautiously, my hand resting on the hilt of my sword. Instinctively, I made the sign of The God on my chest with my other hand. Next to it, a heavy iron-bound door with a small barred window stood securely locked from the inside. I knew this place well. The Weeping Stone. Inside would be the degenerates and filth of Clurak, and all the vice your silver could buy.

"Lovely," Willem mumbled and stepped toward the door. "And there's your cursed bird," he added. The thing is like a terrible omen following us.

Upon the statue's bird-shite covered crown perched the blue-eyed creature, its head cocked, as it looked up on us. I had no heart to tell my friend that this omen was mixed. But it gave me some comfort. I did a double-fingered salute to the creature with my fingers to my forehead and smiled. "Lovely indeed," I agreed with him sarcastically.

I grabbed his arm as he reached for the door. "We do not seek the Weeping Stone," I said. "We seek something else."

"What pray tell? The letter—"

"The forgotten fall," I whispered, my eyes scanning the base of the statue. Hidden in the shadows was a trapdoor, set against the stone wall and barely visible behind The God.

Willem and I exchanged a nod, and together, we heaved the door open, revealing a narrow staircase that descended into the darkness below.

The raven let out a soft caw, as if urging us forward.

With a deep breath, I led the way down the stairs, Willem close behind. The air was damp and musty, the only light the faint glow of a torch flickering in the distance. As we drew closer, the sound of hushed voices reached our ears.

" ... the plan is in motion. The bishop will have his war, and the kingdom will be there for the taking."

I froze, my blood running cold at the words. I recognized the voice from somewhere. Willem's hand gripped my shoulder—a silent warning to stay hidden.

"And what of the King?" another voice asked, a note of trepidation in the tone.

"A necessary sacrifice. His death will be the spark that ignites the flames of chaos, and from the ashes, we will rise and the Crusade will do The God's work. Remember the Second Admonition of the Three Covenants."

I knew the covenants well. All knights did. All Crusaders do. The Second Covenant is Conversion. So often, however, in pursuit of the Second, we have forgotten The First Covenant: Honor. I clenched my fists, anger boiling in my veins. Willem and I crept forward, straining to glimpse the conspirators.

Just as I slid sideways along the blackened corridor, a figure emerged from the shadows in a short side passage across from me, his face shrouded in a hooded cloak. "Ser Aaron," he said, his voice a rasping whisper. "I've been expecting you."

I drew my sword, the blade gleaming in the flickering torchlight. "Who are you?"

The figure chuckled, a dry, humorless sound. "A friend or a foe, depending on your perspective. I have the evidence you seek, proof of the bishop's betrayal. But it comes at a price."

Willem stepped forward, his own weapon at the ready. "We're not here to play games. Hand over the evidence, and we'll be on our way."

The figure shook his head. "It's not that simple. The bishop's men are everywhere, and they'll stop at nothing to keep their secrets safe. You'll have to fight for what you want. Or what I want."

"What do you mean—what you wan–"

I did not fully get the words out when the sound of footsteps echoed from the darkness. The clank of armor and the rasp of steel on leather filled the flickering darkness. Willem and I fell into a defensive stance, ready to face whatever came our way. The shadowed figure stepped behind us.

The two men came on hard. The one of the left was armed with a spear and dressed in worn mail; a sword hung from his waist. The one on the right, came with shield and arming sword.

"I dance with the traitor on the right," Willem said.

"Right, I get the spear," I responded.

There was not much room to move, so this fight would be thrusts and jabs. The Spearman had a certain advantage in that. But, if I could get inside.

I stepped forward, as did Willem. The spearman led, and I feinted left, drawing the fool's spearpoint with me. When he was out of position, I stepped inside his reach, and made to skewer him, relying on Willem to protect my flank from his companion, which he did perfectly. The man on the spearman's left leaned in to finish me on my exposed side, leaving his own flank unwatched, and relying on his shield for protection. But Willem did not strike him. Instead, he hammered the man's sword down and away, drawing him off his footing and allowing me to drive the point of my sword into the spearman's guts. It deflected from his mail, rending the links and ripping an open gash in his armor. The hit sent him reeling against the wall. He released his spear to catch himself, and I pressed my advantage. I shouldered into him, keeping him off balance and smoothly lifting the blade of my weapon into his open throat.

Another swordsman, yet unseen, loomed from the darkness. I was in no position to counter him; my right side turned to him and my sword in the spearman's neck. Nor was Willem in any position to defend me, as he was finishing his opponent. I hoped my steel would stop the strike as I rotated and dodged low to avoid the killing shot. And just as I expected the blow to fall, a piercing cry resonated through the air. The third swordsman instinctively looked up. A tiny black figure hammered into the man's head, emitting a feline hissing noise. As the man fought to knock it away, I took advantage of his distraction and slid my sword through his ribs. He joined his companions on the ground, choking and gurgling as he expired. The cat darted into the darkness.

Before I could even open my mouth or come to grips with what had just occurred, the hooded figure swiftly made his way to the lifeless bodies, his fingers deftly rummaging through their garments and delving into their belt pouches. He quickly reached out and snatched a satchel from one of them. Reaching into it, he pulled out a small, leather-bound scroll casing and pressed it into my hand, then shouldered the satchel.

"Go," he hissed, his voice urgent. "Take the evidence and run."

Willem said, "What is in the bag, Renar–"

"My price, Willem. Let it be the only price I extract."

"We are not your personal assassins," my faithful retainer began. "By The God—"

I grabbed Willem's arm. "Let's be away. We'll figure this out later."

"Yes we will," Willem said, eying Renart, who rushed down the side corridor.

I didn't hesitate, seizing the opportunity to escape.

CHAPTER 5
REVEALATIONS

Sometime later, I sat in Kira's apartments in the central palace, the weight of the scroll was heavy in my hands. I turned it over, my fingers playing across the hardened leather exterior, imagining what might be inside. The flickering candlelight cast a warm glow over the room, but it did little to ease the tension that hung in the air. Willem paced the room, his brow furrowed as we discussed the implications of Renart's actions and the challenges that lay ahead.

"You'll have to open it, ser," he said.

I only nodded. There was this small part of me that thought if I did not open the scroll case, that perhaps whatever terrible thing was inside would not become real.

"Can we trust him?" Willem asked at length, his voice tinged with doubt. "Renart is a shadowy figure, and his motives are unclear. What if this is all part of some larger scheme?"

I sighed, running a hand through my hair. The events of the past few days swirled in my mind, a dizzying array of secrets and betrayals. "We have little choice," I said, looking up at Willem. "The information in this journal, if true, could be the key to exposing the bishop's treachery. We must proceed. But, to your point, my friend, with caution."

Kira entered the room, her face etched with concern. She had been spending more and more time in the King's halls, listening to whispers and gathering what information she could. "I've been hearing disturbing rumors about the bishop's activities within the castle," she said, settling into a chair beside me. "There are whispers of secret meetings and strange alliances. I fear he may move soon. The tension in this place—I can feel it, my brother."

I felt a chill run down my spine at her words. The bishop's influence was far-reaching, and if he truly was conspiring with the Gols, the consequences could be catastrophic. Before I could respond, a knock sounded at the door, startling us all.

Kira rose to answer it, revealing a King's man standing in the hallway. He bowed deeply, his expression serious. "My lady," he said, "A . . . Ser Prenot Baudin is here to see my lord, Aaron. He says it's urgent."

I heard the name, and my heart leaped up into my throat. I rose. The young man was here? I'd rescued the man months before, and he'd watched his own brother betray him and the Crusade. I'd watched Edweene drain the living soul from Dumont in order to survive, something I'd never forget and something I was grateful Ser Prenot had not witnessed. I rose to meet him, and Willem did as well.

Prenot strode into the room a moment later, his face a mask of determination. He looked tired as if he had been riding hard for days without rest. "Ser Aaron," he greeted me, clasping my arm. "I come to aid your mission and redeem my family's honor after my brother's betrayal."

I felt a surge of gratitude at his words. Prenot had suffered at the hands of the Gols, and his brother's treachery had only added to that pain. That he was here, ready to stand with us despite it all, spoke volumes about his character.

"Ser Prenot," I greeted him. "You are welcome here, always. And this is the Captain of my host, Ser Willem, leader of my house's contribution to this Crusade, such as it is," I introduced the two.

"As small as that host may be," Willem quipped. "I have heard of your close call with the Devil and his troupe. I am thankful The God saved you from such a fate."

They made small talk after that. Two men of the same age and disposition they connected well, and soon, we were well-met. As we filled Prenot in on our discoveries, he listened intently, his eyes growing wider with each revelation. I tried to leave my revelations of Edweene, the raven and the cat from the story, but it seemed a point of great excitement to Willem, who added, "Don't forget the cat. A cat verily saved him—from nowhere the little beast leaped upon the enemy's head at the most crucial moment."

Prenot looked pensively at the ceiling. "How did this cat come to be there?" He asked.

"I cannot say, ser, but it was there, and Ser Willem is correct, it might well have kept me from being skewered by steel."

After a moment, Prenot spoke, "During our journey, there were strange occurrences that I haven't been able to shake. A mysterious cat in Caer Gorak, and a raven that seemed to follow us everywhere we went. At first, I dismissed them as coincidences, but now . . . I can't help but feel they are connected somehow. Do you remember, ser?" he asked.

"I remember, Ser. Though I try to forget much of that mission." Beyond that, I kept silent as I understood their genesis, but I had no desire to let Edweene's secret out.

Kira's eyes widened at his words. "A cat?" she asked, leaning forward. "I've seen a cat watching me here in the castle, too. It's always in the shadows, but I swear it's been following me. It has unnerving blue eyes. Quite odd. I thought I was imagining things, but now . . ."

She rose abruptly, a determined look on her face. "Excuse me," she said, moving towards the door. "There's something I need to investigate. I'll be back as soon as I can."

I watched her go, a sense of unease settling in my gut. Kira had always been curious, always seeking answers to the surrounding mysteries. But this was different. The look in her eyes, the urgency in her voice . . . it worried me.

"Kira, wait," I called, rising to my feet. But she was already gone, the door closing behind her with a soft click.

I turned back to Willem and Prenot, my mind racing. "We need more information," I said, tapping the scroll case. "I'll read this lead and see if I can make sense of it's contents. Willem, see what you can learn about the bishop's associates. If he's meeting with anyone suspicious, I want to know about it. Prenot, gather what intelligence you can from your contacts within the Crusade—or, and I know this might be difficult—your family."

Some of his kin blamed him for the loss of Dumont. Those more powerful than we had deigned to tell any of the man's treachery. The risk that carried with the Crusade was dangerous. Dumont and Prenot were from a powerful family, who'd contributed many banners to the endeavor. All this left Prenot in a precarious position. He'd denied the king's orders and had been captured in doing so. Dumont—to all those who did not know he'd turned coat—had gone to rescue him, dying heroically in the doing.

None of that changed our desperate need. After a brief hesitation, I added, "We need to know what they've heard and if anyone else suspects the bishop's treachery."

He nodded, face dark and grim. Willem said, "Agreed, my lord." And with that, we set out on our respective tasks, the weight of our mission heavy on our shoulders.

When they were gone, I considered the scroll case. My heart started a steady staccato that beat against my ribs. I held my breath as I pried open the sealed lid. Inside was another roll of parchment. I pulled it from the case, opened it and read:

*The letters are prepared to send. The Council of
Kings will be ready to support you when the time
comes, when the deed is done. Your people must be
ready to move. The God wills it.*

No address, no names. Nothing. But, I did not
miss the implications of the message. The Council of Kings—the Kings of Bannon, Kivvik, Rogga,
Leonay, and the High Governor of Novik—would
put the crown on someone's head, but only if
the King of Clurak, the Holy Defender, were to
abdicate—or die. The message seemed to con-
firm what was afoot, what our shadowy ally had
intoned. But to whom? Who was ordering this? It
gave little evidence to help us in our quest. Who
has people that could do this? Would do this?
That was the question to be answered. Perhaps
Pernot or Willem would find out more.

Hours later, as the sun dipped below the horizon and the castle fell into shadow, we recon-
vened in Kira's chambers. I of course, had not
left, and had spent my time worrying through
all the dark bastards I knew from my time with
the Dark Men. Perhaps one of them. Rayfe Darkstalker would have been on my list, but I'd killed

him long ago. Who now led the Dark Men? They seemed a likely possibility.

Just as I was rolling up the small document and sliding it back into the case, Kira burst into the room, her face pale and her eyes wide with shock. She was breathing hard as if she had been running, and there was a wild look in her eyes that I had never seen before.

"Aaron," she gasped, gripping my arm. "I have to talk to you, alone."

I looked around the room. "But, we are alone."

Her excitement had me nervous now. My sister was always calm, collected. I rushed to the door and locked it behind her. "No one'll bother us, Kira. What is it?" I asked, my heart pounding in my chest. "What did you find?"

"Edweene," she whispered, her voice barely audible. "I saw her, Aaron. Here in the castle."

My blood ran cold at her words. Edweene. The woman I had killed, the one whose eyes haunted my dreams. The one whose soul I had damned with my own hands. How did she know?

"What?" I asked, my voice hoarse. "How?"

Kira took a deep breath, then recounted her tale. "You were talking of the cat. Like it was some sort of omen. But you knew who—"

"What are you—"

"Let me finish, please, Aaron," she admonished me and I sat down on the foot of the bed.

"I followed the cat," she said. "I had seen it and thought I knew where it was hiding. I wanted to make sure we weren't being listened to as we planned our next move. Anyway, I went there and found a larder in the dungeons, which is a pantry used to keep provisions cool. And there, in the shadows, I witnessed a startling transformation."

My heart climbed into my throat. I coughed, as she stared at me, her eyes wide. She was clutching her hands around her waist. "Kira, I—"

"Aaron, the cat had become a woman, its form shifting and changing like some unholy thing. I could only think it was a creature of devilish ilk. I was going to run, flee the place. But, as I made for the door, she called to me. 'Do not be afraid, Kira,' she said to me. and I was frozen.

I sat back down, put my face in my hands, and mumbled. "Edweene. Kira . . . I can . . . I can—" But, I could not give sound to any words. I struggled to catch my breath. I could not control my racing heart. Suddenly, everything inside me broke.

"She told me everything," Kira said. Her voice trembled. I could not bear to look. "Her death, the dark magic that binds her, and the connection between you. Oh, Aaron, I did not know the weight you carried, the guilt that haunts you."

"Kira," I said. "It is more than that. I . . . I something is growing inside me. Has been for many years. I think of little else but Edweene. And yet, she is an abomination. A demon. But, I am drawn—"

I felt as if the ground had shifted beneath my feet. Edweene, here in the castle. The secrets of my past laid bare before my sister, the one person I had tried so hard to protect from the horrors of this war. I wanted to be angry, to lash out at Kira for putting herself in danger. Or was it myself I was angry with? I had hidden the darkest, most vile parts of my life, and I had buried away my sacrilege and now . . . I was ashamed. I looked up at her. But looking into her eyes, I saw only compassion and a fierce determination.

"Edweene is not your enemy," Kira said softly, taking my hand. "No is she an abomination. She is bound by some dark ritual. True. But, she has no more ability to control it than the wind, or the earth. The God would find no guilt there."

"Kira, I know you are trying—"

"From what I can tell, she made you who you are Aaron. This man bent on redeeming The God's house. This good person who sits here before me. She is a part of you, Aaron."

"I murdered her," Kira. "You don't understand, how this gnaws at my guts, and squeezes my heart as if it would have me killed."

"I do not understand, Aaron. That is true. But, I do know you did not murder her. You saved her. And she you."

The tears were rolling down her cheeks, now. And I could not stop the welling in my own. She sat next to me and wrapped her arms around me. I did likewise.

She continued, "Aaron, I think she is crucial in this fight. You must trust in the strength of your bond, Aaron. Let her help you. Bring her in."

I closed my eyes, letting Kira's words wash over me. She was right, of course. I had been running from my past for too long, letting guilt and fear cloud my judgment. If we were to have any hope of defeating the bishop and his allies, I needed to embrace every weapon at my disposal. But she was so pitched against Gavreaux, and I could not help thinking the Passage knight was an important ally.

Even if that weapon was a ghost from my past, an abominable lych?

Taking a deep breath, I squared my shoulders and met Kira's gaze. "Thank you," I said, my voice rough with emotion. "For everything."

She smiled, squeezing my hand. "We're in this together, Aaron. All of us."

A knock on the door and a jiggling of the handle pulled us apart. A feeling of loss came to me as we parted. There was little comfort in this dark land, and moments with my sister were scarce. I lived in fear of being found out for my indiscre-

tions and guilt for my actions. It was a moment
of comfort that was rarely realized.

"My lord, are you within?" Prenot's voice muffled through the door.

"Perhaps we'd best not go in. All the courtly
maids in the castle. Aaron was quite the favorite
back home . . ." Willem's incessant humor followed along, and they laughed.

"Kira smiled at me. You were, you know." She
laughed a moment, too, as I rose to open the
door, shaking my head. Levity in this darkness
was welcome, even if at my expense.

Together, Willem and Prenot came into the
room.

I took a moment to compose myself before
facing the others.

"Is everything alright?" Willem asked, always
perceptive. His gaze darted between us.

I took a deep breath, choosing my words carefully. "There have been some developments," I
said, my voice steady despite the turmoil within.
"Kira has discovered that an old acquaintance of
mine, Edweene, is here in the castle."

Prenot's brow furrowed. "Edweene? From Caer Gorak?"

"Yes. She has a complicated history with the Crusades and the Gols. I believe she may have valuable information that could aid our cause."

Willem leaned forward, his interest piqued. "This is the woman you dream about. Hah. The plot thickens, Aaron. When can I meet this deadly heartbreaker? And . . . more importantly, can she be trusted?"

I hesitated, weighing the question in my mind. "I believe so," I said at last. "But her situation is complex. For now, let's just say that she has reasons to help us, but . . . there are risks."

Kira spoke up then, her voice firm. "I have arranged for us to meet with Edweene in secret, away from prying eyes. She has agreed to share what she knows and to offer her assistance in any way she can."

Prenot and Willem exchanged a glance, their expressions a mix of curiosity and apprehension. "You know her, too?" Willem asked, incredulous.

"We've only just met. Accidentally. She was . . . watching us, let's just say, and we made contact."

"Ah . . ." Prenot left the vague response alone. "Very well," he said, "if you believe this Edweene can be an asset to our cause, then we will trust your judgment."

I felt a surge of gratitude for their faith in me, even in the face of so many unknowns. "Thank you," I said, "both of you. I know there are still many questions to be answered, but I have a feeling Edweene may hold information that could be key to unlocking the truth behind the bishop's plans, or she can lead us to those who might."

CHAPTER 6
A BAG OF SILVER

The morning sun crept through the narrow windows of Kira's chambers, casting a warm glow across the room. Prenot, Willem, and I sat around the table, our faces somber as we discussed our next steps. We'd slept on the floor last night, despite the discomfort it might bring Kira from the court when they found out men were attending her in her apartments. Of course, her brother was not an issue, but two young single men like Prenot and Willem might raise an eyebrow or two.

When I brought it up last night, she'd said, "I care little for the rumors of people I barely know—certainly not more than the well-being of those set to defeat godless turncoats."

Whatever the case, we'd reconciled the potential loss of her honor to her demands, and now we sat around her small table. It was early and my stomach was grumbling for breakfast. But that would have to wait. I furrowed my brow and said to them, "I can't shake the feeling that Maester Aldric is involved in the bishop's schemes. The way he looked at me when we arrived, the smugness in his voice . . . it was as if he knew something we didn't."

Prenot nodded, his expression grim. "I've heard whispers about Aldric's ambitions and his close relationship with the bishop. If anyone knows the truth, it's him, I would wager. He has had the king's ear for a long time. And he was close to my brother. Indeed, he served as a tutor of sorts when he was young with my family's estate."

"We need to find out what he's up to," Willem agreed. "But we can't afford to be reckless. If Aldric suspects we're onto him, he could disappear or, worse, alert the bishop."

I leaned forward and narrowed my eyes to make a point. "I say we split up. Prenot, you stay here in the castle and monitor Kira. Your family is on the court. It will seem natural. And protect her.

"Aaron . . . I need no such protection."

She was glaring at me as if I'd insulted her. Though it was not my intent, I perhaps did. I was worried about her, of course. Though she was a hardy soul, she had not faced steel like we Crusaders had. Still, she likely didn't need Prenot's protection. Kira could handle the court dandies and anyone not bent on cutting her throat. But she lacked training in blade or mace. What if an assassin came upon her? Someone looking to settle a score with me or apply leverage to get me to stop my investigation. Kira was the leverage that they would use to do so. And Prenot was a competent combatant, a knight—and of noble blood. Killers, even committed ones, would pause before striking him.

"Kira, please. This is no judgement on you. I have the most faith in you, of all people. I only ask that you keep his sword nearby. Ser Prenot is a valiant warrior and skilled with a sword—"

"I can speak for myself, ser," he interjected. "I will not overstep my bounds, my lady. And I will not undermine your position here. I will merely be at your service," he said. "Use me as you will."

It seemed to satisfy her, and she nodded. "Thank you, ser. Alright," she said.

"Ok, Kira, see if you are able to gather any more information from the servants or the guards. Willem and I will investigate Aldric and the Dark Men."

Willem cleared his throat, his expression thoughtful. "I have been thinking," he said. "It has been some time since I've checked in on our formations. I should return to the camp and make sure everything is in order. We don't want any surprises when the time comes to act. And they no doubt miss me, and you, of course. Sergeant Deres will have them in good order, but they grow weary and restless. It is not good to be away so long."

I considered this for a moment, then nodded. "You are right, Willem. We need to be prepared for anything. Go to the camp, rally the men, and make sure they see you. Hear you. We have not abandoned them. And, Willem . . ."

"Yes, my lord."

"Make sure Sergent Deres has them ready to move at a moment's notice if it comes to it."

"I will, ser," he finished.

"And that he understands the import of what we do, here. I would know his loyalty on the matter."

With our plans set, the three of us went our separate ways. I set out into the city, my cloak pulled tight around my shoulders to ward off the chill morning air. I silently maneuvered through the streets, relapsing into the behaviors I had gained during my past as a Dark Man. My eyes scanned the crowds for any sign of Maester Aldric, staying in those places I knew he frequented. He was a man of disreputable tastes but not so stupid as to find his way to a den of shite like the Weeping Stone. No. He frequented the back doors of the discrete brothels in Hightown and spice houses of the Silver Road—more likely, he procured his vices in the same places he bought the strange mixtures for his potions and elixirs, which made finding him a matter of time, not an aimless search.

It didn't take long to spot the Maester, his distinctive robes marking him out among the throng of merchants, wealthy landed, and nobles who perused the Silver Road—or simply the Silver. I tailed him at a distance, watching as Aldric wound his way through the crowded marketplace and thoroughfare known for its active shops and vendors seeking products and materials for their trade and manufactured goods.

As the sun climbed higher in the sky, Aldric's path took him to a secluded corner of Hightown, away from the bustle of the Silver, but not so far as to prevent rapidly dissolving into the crowd. Only one street and a dark alley away from the busy boulevard, I watched from the shadows as the Maester approached a hooded figure, their faces obscured by the deep cowls of their cloaks.

The two men exchanged a few words, then the hooded figure passed a heavy pouch that jingled with coin to Aldric, who tucked it quickly into his robes. With a final nod, the two parted ways, Aldric heading back towards the castle while the hooded figure disappeared into the labyrinthine alleys.

My heart raced as I watched the exchange, my mind whirling with possibilities. What was in that scroll, and who was the hooded figure? Moving swiftly, I tried to follow this new entrant into the conspiracy, but the man was quick and seemed to know the city's back streets like the back of his hand. Despite my best efforts, I soon lost sight of my quarry, the trail going cold in the twisting maze of buildings and shadowed courtyards as he made his way out of Hightown towards the merchant's ward, heading toward the Temple of Tears.

Frustrated, I made my way back to the castle. As I slipped through the gates, I couldn't shake the feeling that I was being watched, a prickling sensation on the back of my neck that set my nerves on edge. Somewhere, I heard a flutter of wings. My heightened senses warned me of movement ahead. I slowed my pace and watched the darkness closely. Even so, I almost did not notice the figure waiting for me in a secluded corner of the grounds, half-hidden in the shadow of a low palace palisade.

"Aaron," a voice whispered, and I froze. My hand shot to the hilt of my sword. Then the figure stepped forward, and my breath caught in my throat. It was Edweene, her blue eyes glinting in the fading light.

"What are you doing here?" I hissed, glancing around to make sure we were alone. "It's not safe for you to be seen." But what I wanted to do was run to her, hold her—a closeness that always seems to overcome me when she is near, a tie based on sacrifice and shared pains. But regret and guilt tinged it, regardless of what Kira said. I stopped myself and punched my hands into my sword belt.

Edweene's lips twitched into a smirk. "I'm touched by your concern," she said. "But I assure you, my blades are always ready to take care of any who would threaten me."

I shook my head, torn between frustration and a familiar, cursed sense of relief at seeing her again. "What do you want, Edweene?"

"Are you not grateful to see me?" She asked rhetorically. She knew how I felt. We'd shared much these last few months. If I could spend a thousand years with one person, it would be Edweene. But such a thing was a foolish, doomed notion. Her expression sobered, and she took a step closer. "I want what you want," she said. "To stop the bishop and his allies from plunging this kingdom into a war whose end cannot be predicted. The Gols and their allies outnumber the Crusade by many fold. It would be a long and bloody thing and might well extract much blood and silver from the northern and eastern kingdoms . . .

I kept staring at her, incredulous. When had she grown concern for the nations that had abandoned her, here?

She laughed. "That's the right answer, my rehearsed answer. But, in the end, I suppose, Aaron, if you look through all of that, I came for you. I live on regardless of who fights this war . . . and who dies in it."

Her words resonated inside me this time. She was here for me. It was not a lie. She did not need to be here; had no pressing urgency. She was already beyond what petty needs came with life. Her life was transcendent, I suppose. But her need for vengeance ran as hot as mine. "And Gavreaux?" I asked, my voice tight. "Do you still seek retribution against him?"

Edweene's eyes flashed, and for a moment, I saw the depth of her pain and anger. "Gavreaux abandoned me," she said. "Left me to die—or worse—at the hands of the Gols. I cannot forget that, nor can I forgive it."

I sighed, running a hand through my hair. "I understand your desire for justice," I said. "But Gavreaux could be a powerful ally in this fight. We need all the help we can get."

Edweene was silent for a long moment, her gaze distant. "I have set aside my vendetta against Gavreaux for now," she said at last. "But only because the threat we face is greater than any personal grievance. It is like our excursion to find your young friend, the brave Ser Prenot. I put aside my desires for revenge simply for you, Aaron. I have endless time to find my justice. I do not have endless time . . " she looked down and the ground and shuffled her feet a bit. Then she looked up at me, and our eyes met. "I do not have endless time with you, Aaron. That is my dilemma."

I nodded and looked down again, unable to meet her piercing eyes for long. She carried a lot of pain. And she had no one to carry it with her. She was alone in every way possible. The Gols wished to enslave her, and . . . well, those that served The God found her an abomination, a thing of the Devil. To say I was relieved to have at least a temporary truce was an understatement. But the admission of her longing was beyond what she'd ever said to me. How must it be to be so alone? It was something that would pain her greatly to speak of, so filled with pride was she. So, I went on with the topic at hand. I reached out, took her arm, and guided her deeper into the shadows. "Tell me, Edweene, what do you know about assassins in the city?" I asked. "There is a plot afoot, and the bishop is at the heart of it. It is more than the ham-fisted attempt to start a war with Prenot's retinue and my murder."

Edweene's expression turned grim. "There is no such thing as 'assassins' as you speak of them, Aaron. You know this. Once, people would have seen you as such. Assassins here are little more than mercenaries, doing what others do, but for profit. Is this what you mean? Or are you seeking zealots of The God, or the Old Gods, or men of knightly virtue who would kill for a cause?

She was so confounding. Challenging me at every turn. My time in the Dark Men was a response to the futility of armored formations and mass combat. I'd figured we could end the Crusade more quickly, by stealth and dagger, than by mass slaughter. It was a fool's notion. One did not stop the other.

"Edweene," I said, "You know what I mean. Have you seen—"

"I know what you mean, Aaron. But my point holds true. Who would kill for this thing? This is where we start, no? I saw you today. You were on the right track. I don't know who is plotting this thing, ser. I can say that with certainty. But I have my suspicions. This Maester of yours seems connected to many factions. I've watched him in the court, as—"

"Yes. The cat," I said.

"Correct. The cat," she laughed. "Your sister is smarter than you, Aaron. But not by much. She is also less driven by external virtues and more by emotional attachments."

"Is this good?"

"They both have their benefits. I think I could have hurt her badly, though, or perhaps manipulated her, for she is too tied to you emotionally. She would believe a lych if that creature carried an abominable torch for you."

I breathed deeply. This conversation was going places I did not wish it to go. But I dug the hole a little deeper, anyway. "And does this lych . . . carry a torch?"

"Back to the matter at hand, shall we?" she said and smiled that sardonic smile of hers. This creature was exasperating. "I have followed all these foul people. Your King, excluded, of course, that man seems a shiny thing among excrement. You would do well to protect him. All of the others could be who we seek. Maybe they all are, including the family of our good friend Prenot. You know they have close ties with the bishop, do you not? It seems it was not simply Dumont but the boy's mother, the Earless Monae."

My mind raced, the puzzle getting more and more complex as I looked at the scattered pieces. "This is new . . . about Prenot's family. I will have to think on this. But I know Maester Aldric is involved somehow," I said. "I saw him meeting with a hooded figure earlier, exchanging some sort of bag, likely coin."

Edweene's eyes narrowed. "You know? Or you think?"

"Fine, Edweene, I think. But my instincts are right on this matter. I am sure of it."

"I don't doubt it. Aldric is a snake," she spat. "From what I can tell, in my short time here, he is close to the bishop, whispering poison in the King's ear. But don't forget the others. I think you may be right . . he is a connection between all these parties. Tooleb, Transom, Prenot's mother, the distinguished Earless, the rest . . . even Gavreaux, if you were willing to look there."

"How do you know all this?"

"A cat has access to places no person can go. And they are free to roam, you know. We hunt the dreaded rat . . . enemy of ladies in all the lands." She laughed a bit. "No one suspects a cat."

I did my best to ignore the reference to her transmutations. I still struggled with the heretical powers that came with her undeath, and something were better to acknowledge and ignore, I figured. Easier, I suppose, than accepting who I felt such closeness to. I pushed past her baseless implication of Gavreaux and went on. "We have to move faster. We have but a day or two," I said. "Gather more evidence, protect those who are most at risk."

Edweene nodded, her face set with determination. "I will continue my investigations," she said. "I have ways of influencing the righteous . . . and the not-so-righteous. I will see what I can find."

I shivered at the thought, remembering when she drained Dumont of his life's spirit. It was ungodly and unnerving to know the man's soul would never find The God—a thought I reckoned best not considered. The things I accepted for my connection to this creature would be the death of me, physically or spiritually. "Be careful," I said, surprising myself with the depth of my concern. "If the bishop discovers what we're doing . . ."

Edweene's smile was a flash of teeth in the darkness. "I am always careful," she said. "But I appreciate the sentiment."

With a final nod, she melted back into the shadows, leaving me alone with my thoughts. I took a deep breath, trying to calm my racing heart, then headed back towards the castle, my mind already turning over the next steps in our plan.

Chapter 7
A Gathering Storm

I found my sister in her chambers, sitting in front of her mirror and brushing out her long hair. She looked up as I entered, her brow furrowed with concern. "Hello, brother," she said. I caught her eyes in the mirror and tried to maintain a certain modicum of calm. It, of course, did not fool her. Her eyes narrowed slightly, and she tugged at a knot in her hair as she spoke. "Aaron? What's wrong?" She always looked so tranquil, even when we were children. I was always looking for something more as a child, agitated, pensive, and impatient. And she seemed so content, regardless of what assailed us.

I closed the door behind me and approached her. I kept my voice low and inserted as much urgency as I could without looking—or sounding—like a fool. It was not as though I could control it. The events had taken on a life of their own and carried their own weight, their own urgency. "I may have uncovered something, Lady Kira. It is . . . it is something that may add more weight to our mission."

She listened as I recounted my conversation with Edweene, particularly her warning about the Earless Monae's potential involvement in the conspiracy and the Maester's connection to all of our potential conspirators.

"The Earless?" Kira's eyes widened. "But why would she betray the King? Her family has always been loyal to the crown and, more importantly, The God."

"I don't know," I admitted. "But Edweene seems to think she may be involved somehow. She touches on so much of this: Dumont, Prenot, she's close to both the Maester and the King. There are many ties there. I think we need to keep a close eye on her, Kira. Watch for any suspicious behavior or meetings with the bishop or Aldric."

Kira nodded, her expression grave. "I cannot believe this is so, Aaron. We should be careful not to leap to conclusions. But I understand the import. I will do what I can to monitor her movements and interactions. My position in the court is not a thing to grant me favors, but it still should allow me some level of access."

I placed a hand on her shoulder, my grip firm. "Be careful, Kira. If the Earless is involved, she's likely to be just as dangerous as the bishop himself. She nearly sacrificed her own son on a mission that resulted in him being captured by the Gols. We can't afford to underestimate her."

Just then, the door to Kira's chambers swung open, and Prenot strode in. Kira and I quickly changed the subject, trying to hide our true discussion.

"Ah, Prenot," I said, forcing a smile. "We were just discussing the latest news from the Crusader camp. Or lack thereof. Any word from Willem?"

Prenot's eyes narrowed, clearly suspicious of our sudden shift in conversation. "No," he said slowly. "In fact, that's what I came to talk to you about."

I exchanged a glance with Kira, my heart sinking. "What do you mean?"

"I saw Maester Aldric returning to the palace earlier," Prenot explained. "He was in a great hurry, stopping only to whisper something to a guard and his companion before rushing off to his chambers. I've never seen him so agitated."

Of course, I assumed the Maester would come back to the palace, so his presence did not surprise me, nor did his state of mind after his meeting with the stranger. I said as much, "It does not surprise me. I am interested in what you saw when he arrived, ser. I followed him today. He met with a shadowy man in Hightown, off the Silver, where the meeting could be hidden. I tried to follow his dark conspirator. But I lost him in the city. Perhaps that is what could have excited him so much. He left with a pouch of coin from the meeting. I would like to know what that was to be used for."

"Hmm ... that adds some interesting information to what I witnessed. It helps to make some sense. But whether it is the reason for his actions, I don't know. I can say that he passed a similar bag to the guard," Prenot admitted.

What did interest me, however, was the Maester's interaction with the guards. I could not help wondering if it was related. "Do you know who this other footman was?" I asked.

"I did not recognize the man. But he rushed off, heading to the front of the palace gates. Where he was going in such a hurry is anyone's guess." He shrugged, then went on, "Also, Ser Willem should have returned from the camp by now. His absence is troubling, given the circumstances."

I nodded, my mind already racing with possibilities. "You are correct. His mission should not have taken this entire day. Should send a messenger? If something's happened . . ."

"No, Aaron. You two should be gone. I will deal with the other matter," Kira interjected to the conversation.

Prenot and I gathered our gear and set out, then set out for the crusader camp. We went on foot to avoid notice. Taking our horses from the stables might have alerted someone to our leaving. We strode quickly for the Crusader camp. The streets of Clurak were dark and empty; the only sound was the clattering of our horses' hooves on the cobblestones.

Passed under the city gates and through the barbican, saying salutations to the guards as we did. Once outside, we shortly entered the shanties of the follower camp's emporium, where many services were supplied to the would-be holy soldiers and their camps. It was dark, and we'd just passed a ramshackle construct used for a smithy when a sudden movement caught my eye. I held up a hand, signaling for Prenot to stop. "We're not alone," I whispered.

No sooner had the words left my mouth than five assassins emerged from the shadows, their blades glinting in the moonlight. Four wore dark cloaks and hoods, their faces obscured by masks painted like devils and gorgons. One stood ahead, garbed in mail and carrying a shield and sword. He wore an open-faced helmet and smiled widely at us.

As one, Ser Prenot and I drew our swords.

The assassins circled us, their movements quick and precise. "Surrender, and your deaths will be quick," the lead warrior demanded, as though that was a viable option for a knight of the Crusade.

"I do not live for a quick death, traitor," I spat. I tightened my grip on my sword.

"You," Prenot spouted, as he pointed his blade at the leader. "I saw you in the palace with that serpent, Aldric. What is your—"

The assassins surged forward, around their armored leader, blades flashing and cutting short Prenot's words. We leaned into the attack, stepping forward. I deflected the first sword quickly and drove my elbow into the killer's face. He stepped back, groaning, hand grasping at his broken nose, as the other came in hard. I rotated in time to deflect his sword and sidestepped to keep him between me and his companion, hoping to limit the weapons that they could bring against me. From the corner of my eye, I could see Prenot equally pressed. Despite their first foolish rush, they were not unskilled, and they outnumbered us.

They pressed the attack again. One assassin slipped past my guard, and his blade slid across my chain sleeve, but failing to penetrate the gambeson beneath. A few inches closer, though, and he would have laid my throat open. I gritted my teeth and retaliated with a swift thrust along his extended blade, and spun it out as I drove in, two hands on the hilt. My sword bit deep, and the satisfying resistance of meat and bone behind his own padded surcoat told me my sword found its mark. The man fell back, dropped his own weapon, then collapsed to the ground.

Beside me, Prenot cried out in pain. I turned to see him staggering back, his hand pressed against his side. Blood seeped between his fingers, staining his tunic a dark crimson. I lunged forward, placing myself between Prenot and the assassins. "Stay behind me," I ordered, my voice strained with exertion.

"You chose your side, my lord," one assassin taunted Prenot. "You chose against your brother. Now, we reconcile that."

Prenot's eyes widened, his face paling at the implication. "My brother? What are you talking about?"

The assassin laughed, a cruel, mocking sound. "The Earless suffers for your failures."

I felt a surge of anger at the mention of the Lady Monae. More evidence that she might be involved. And if she truly was involved in this conspiracy, then Prenot's own mother had betrayed him and sent assassins for him. It seemed mad. I pushed forward, doing my best to keep Prenot behind me while the assassin who had struck him leaned in and deflected my clumsy attack. As I danced sideways, I narrowly avoided being skewered from his riposte and slipped my hilt up to deflect his precise attack.

He laughed at me and taunted me with a wave of his sword.

Now, three stood against me. Behind them, their commander turned and disappeared into the dusk.

Prenot leaned heavily against a nearby wall, his breath coming in ragged gasps. "Aaron," he whispered, his voice weak. "You must go. Leave me and find Willem."

"Never," I growled, standing protectively over my fallen comrade. "I did not pull you from that Golish cesspit to see you murdered by traitorous dogs in our own camp. I won't abandon you, Prenot. Not now, never."

The assassins closed in, their blades glinting with the promise of death. I knew then that I would likely perish here, in this darkened place, far from the home I ostensibly came here to defend for the Star of the God, and the people I loved. Die before I solved this mystery and brought this plot to an end. But I would die with my honor intact, defending my friend and the cause I believed in.

"Bring on your steel, cowards. Let us see which of us dies on this street," I jeered.

But again, The God was with me. As I prepared myself for the final onslaught, a shout rang out from the darkness. "Aaron! Prenot!"

I dare not turn for the risk of being struck down. But, from my periphery, I could see Willem advancing towards us, a contingent of six or eight

Crusaders who wore my livery at his back. They crashed into the assassins like an iron wave, their shields leading the way.

The battle was fierce but short-lived. With Willem and the Crusaders' aid, we quickly dispatched the remaining assassins, leaving their bodies littering the blood-soaked ground.

The leader was nowhere to be seen.

I kneeled beside Prenot, helping him to sit up. "Are you alright?" I asked. It was difficult to keep the concern from my voice. Confidence is what the boy needed, not my emotional weakness.

Prenot nodded, wincing as he pressed a hand to his wound. "I'll live, thanks to you and Willem."

"You came at just the right moment, ser," I said to Willem as he approached, his face grim. "My gratitude to you."

"I was returning with our man, Deres, when we heard the commotion from the camp," he explained. "I feared the worst when I saw the fighting. Deres was quick to react. He is a good man."

"The God willed it," I said, clasping his arm in gratitude. "A moment later, and Prenot and I would have been cut down."

"As you say, it was the will of The God," Deres said, and made the Star on his chest. "Who are these conspirators who would attack my lord so brazenly?"

"A good question," I said. "I believe that Ser Prenot here recognized one of them . . . but he made good his escape, unfortunately. They spoke of the Earless, Prenot's own mother."

"Impossible, is it not? An unfounded implication?"

I was about to respond, as we helped Prenot to his feet, Willem's gaze fell upon one of the fallen assassins. He kneeled down, his brow furrowing as he examined the body.

"What is it?" I asked, noticing his troubled expression.

Willem pointed to a partially obscured tattoo on the assassin's neck. "Look," he said, his voice low and urgent. "The tear-shaped device of the Knights of Tears, though someone has attempted to burn it off."

"By The God. The Tears. You are right.:" I felt a chill run through me at the sight. The Knights took an oath to protect the Holy Land and the King himself—or the Temple, I should say. The difference was not insubstantial. If they were involved in this conspiracy, then indeed Knight Commander Transom was involved—or had lost control of his Order.

"And my mother," Prenot said, his voice a pain-filled whisper. "What of her?" His hand trembled as he pressed it against his wound, his face a mask of pain and disbelief. I could only imagine the turmoil raging within him at the thought of his own mother's betrayal. Family was much to Prenot, and, after his brother's betrayal, that the Earless could be involved in a plot against the King and the Crusade must have shaken him to his very core. That would mean she'd sacrifice him as well. All for the damnable war.

"Prenot," I whispered, placing a hand on his shoulder. "We don't know the full story yet. There may be more to this than meets the eye."

He nodded, swallowing hard as he met my gaze. "I know. But if it's true, if she really has turned against us . . . And she sent me to die. I don't know if I can bear it."

"We need to get back to the palace," I said, my mind racing with the implications of this discovery. "Deres, can Willem and I rely on you to ready the men, keep them sharp, prepared for our call? The King—and the Crusade—may well depend on it.

"Yes my lord," he stood tall. "Of course, my lord. I stand for The God and those turned coat against him will feel our steel. The steel of River-shire."

"Good man," Willem said, and I nodded my affirmation.

"Lady Kira needs to know what we've learned, and we must learn from her. Then we must plan our next move carefully. Willem, take one man and usher Prenot to the camp infirmary. Watch over him. I would not have him taken to the Temple hospital overseen by the Knights of Tears, knowing what we know."

"I am f—" Prenot began.

"No, my Lord. You are not. You bleed like a leaking wineskin. Don't kill yourself for a knight's pride, young Prenot. Better to die swinging than leaking to death from stubbornness. Besides, no one will want to talk to you. I can smell your bowels from here." Willem corrected him, and wrinkled up his nose, his irreverent joking falling on deaf ears.

He loosed a bit of an unhinged laugh and shook his head. "But, the Lady Monae, my mother, must be confronted. I must find out—"

"I will do so, ser," I said. "You must deal with that wound. If not, it will surely kill you. No more conversation, my lords. The God's time is limited, and we must do his bidding."

Supporting Prenot between them, Willem and a private soldier carried him away toward one of the camp infirmaries—the closest to my banner's bivouac. Sergeant Deres took the remaining soldiers back to our encampment, and I made way back through the city streets toward the palace.

A wheel of dark images spun inside my head. Images of the near-mortal wound inflicted upon my companion, the Earless Monae, the Knights of Tears, and the bishop himself. All these things, all these people who were in this web of treachery. It would take all our strength and cunning to unravel it—and more so to face it in the end.

But here I was, alone again. And as I neared the palace gates, I couldn't shake the feeling that we were all walking into a gathering storm, one that would test our resolve and our faith like never before.

CHAPTER 8
REVELATIONS

As I went through the palace halls, the weight of the revelations about the Earless Monae's potential involvement in the conspiracy pressed down on me. The intricate tapestries and lavish furnishings blended into a blur as my mind was fixated on the task before me. I had to confront Lady Monae and hear the truth from her own lips. I stopped at Kira's apartment and knocked on the door.

When she answered, I could not keep the look of despair from my face. She reached out and pulled me in, slipping the door shut behind me.

"Are you well, ser?" she asked.

I choked on the words, "Yes. I am well."

She laughed sardonically. Then she pulled me close to her, wrapping her silk-clad arms around me and my filthy, bloody surcoat, mail and all. "You are the worst of liars, Aaron. The absolute worst."

I coughed, still breathing hard from the fight, and climbed up the city's central hill to where the palace castle stood atop the cliffs overlooking the sea. I pulled away, not to avoid her embrace, but to look in her face. "Ser Prenot has taken a sword to the belly. Assassins," I said.

Her eyes welled up, but she fought off the tears. "Prenot. Is that his . . ." her hand went to my chest, and her fingers touched the mess on my surcoat tentatively . . . "blood?"

"Some of it," I said. I pulled her hand away as though touching it would somehow corrupt her perfectness with the taint of my life. I was suddenly angry with myself for bringing her into the is world of shite. And, I selfishly had forgotten that she was not used to seeing blood, and leavings of battle. When it was your own or that of your friends, it could be most discomfiting.

"Some is the enemies. More of them fell than us."

"Who did this?" she asked, her eyes steely.

"I do not know. Prenot recognized the leader, as a guard that was here in the palace. The one he said met with the Maester when he returned from the Silver. One—" I couldn't finish. I had to take a deep breath and gather my thoughts.

"One, what, Aaron?" She said in that motherly tone she could level on me when I did the wrong things.

I answered by instinct, as is my way with her, "One assassin wore some semblance of the symbol of the Knights of Tears . . . and one . . ."

"Go on."

"One spoke of the Earless, Prenot's mother. I fear it is as Edweene had said, as we had discussed earlier."

She became a dust dervish of activity after that. She rose, straightened up the last of her hair, tucking it into place, grabbed my arm and rushed me out the door.

"We're going to her now," she said. "We'll hear from her mouth."

As we approached the Earless' chambers, my heart was stony, and I had resolved myself to murder or something only a little less extreme. I would have some semblance of vengeance for what had been done to the young knight. He had suffered terribly this last year. Now, his family?

Kira placed a hand on my arm, stopping me as we strode down the corridor. We'd been quiet, and I knew she could feel the rage festering inside me.

"Aaron," she said, her voice low and urgent.

I turned to face her. I furrowed my brow and narrowed my eyes. "What is it, Kira? You are right. We need to speak with the Earless as soon as possible. And maybe—"

Kira's eyes searched mine, her expression a mix of concern and determination. "I know, but we need to be smart about this. The Earless is a powerful woman with a lot of influence and a lot to lose. We can't just barge in there and start making accusations."

I sighed, running a hand through my hair. "Kira . . . the killer, as much as said, she sent him to kiss her own on. Prenot is a knight, and a nobleman. His lineage . . . it is everything. He has seen it soiled. The thought of his own mother being involved in this treachery . . ."

Kira squeezed my arm, her touch gentle but firm. "I understand, Aaron. But we need to approach this with a clear head and an open mind. The Earless may have her own reasons for her actions, and we need to listen. Aaron, she may not even see us. We are the lowest of the court here."

I nodded, taking a deep breath to calm my discontinuous thoughts. "She'll see us, Kira. I saved her son, if that means anything to her. But, I also struck down her other son. If she is a conspirator, she may know that too. It was not Gol or Gorgon. It was me . . . me and Edweene," I pushed away the memory of Edweene feeding her unnatural hunger on the traitor knight. "Or, perhaps she does. I don't know. Even so, you're right, as usual," I said with a small grimace. "What do you suggest?"

Kira's expression turned thoughtful. "Let me take the lead in the conversation. I may be able to establish a rapport with the Earless, to make her feel more at ease. And if she sees that we're not there to judge but to understand, she may be more willing to open up to us."

I felt a surge of anger at Kira's words and could not contain myself, though I must admit, I did not try very hard. I said, "Kira, I am here to judge. This cannot be allowed to—"

"Aaron, stop." She put her open palm in my face. "Stop, brother. I know you are angry. And your honor is offended. But you are not thinking this through. If you go in there, waving your sword about and making threats, all that will happen is losing our biggest lead, and perhaps worse, even arrest. We cannot be foolish here. Monae is important, but there are more important ogres to slay here. Much more important. You will lose it all with that temper of yours."

I did not know what to say to her sudden assertion of control. I simply stared. And nodded. Sometimes with the Lady Kira, you were best to nod and agree. I did just that. Remember, Kira I said, "Prenot's honor must remain intact. He has been wronged, and I intend to set it right . . ."

Kira let a small smile play at the corners of her mouth. "I wouldn't expect anything less from you, Aaron. But remember, we're here to gather information, not to start a fight. The Earless is not our enemy, at least not yet. When the time is right, you can reclaim his honor . . . and yours."

I sighed, the weight of our task settling heavily on my shoulders. "I know, Kira. It's just . . . with everything that's happened, I trust no one . . . but you." *And Edweene*, I thought. But I left that unsaid. I hoped she was with us now, somewhere in the shadows, if things came to bloodletting.

Kira's eyes softened, and she reached out to take my hand in hers. "Thank you. You can trust me, Aaron. And you can trust in the strength of our bond, as siblings and as allies in this fight. We'll get through this together, no matter what."

I squeezed her hand, drawing strength from it. "Thank you, Kira."

Kira grinned, a mischievous glint in her eye. "Probably get yourself into even more trouble than usual," she teased.

I laughed, feeling some of the tension drain from my body. "Likely," I admitted.

Kira's expression turned serious once more. "Are you ready?" she asked, tilting her head towards the Earless' chambers.

I nodded, squaring my shoulders and taking a deep breath. "As ready as I'll ever be. Let's do this."

We found the Earless in her sitting room, surrounded by the trappings of her station—all cherry wood and silk-covered furniture and heavy tapestries that reminded me of home hung from the walls, keeping the large room warm and comfortable. A fire burned in the hearth, and oil lamps lit the place from their gleaming mounts on the walls. The Earless sat at a large, ornately carved desk, surrounded by stacks of papers and maps. A great window opened from her wing, looking out onto the Sea of Sorrows. The vast sea was dark, and the moon hung low over the black water, reflecting an eerie blue light made the arched window look like an entrance to the Devil's world.

Two imposing soldiers flanked the open arched entrance, their hands resting on the hilts of their swords. They stepped forward as we approached, their expressions wary. They took in my bloodied armor and disheveled appearance with narrowed, questioning eyes.

"State your business," one of them said, his voice gruff and unyielding.

I drew myself up to my full height, meeting his gaze steadily. "Ser Aaron of Rivershire and Lady Kira, here to speak with the Earless Monae on a matter of great urgency."

The guard hesitated, glancing at his companion. Before they could respond, the Earless' voice rang out from within the chamber. "Let them pass, Ser Torren. I know this man. He saved my son, your lord. And . . . I know this lady. I have seen her these last two days in court. Though I have yet to make her acquaintance. I will hear what they have to say. I am sure they mean me no harm, despite . . . ahem . . . his appearance."

The guards stepped aside, allowing us to enter. She looked up as we approached, her expression guarded. The earless was an imposing woman, clad in the finest, rose-colored silk, brocaded dress. She was tall and lovely in a timeless way. Her blonde hair was braided and curled up on her head. She smiled disarmingly at us as we entered, which put me even more on my guard. "Ser Aaron, Lady Kira. To what do I owe this unexpected visit?"

Kira stepped forward, her voice calm and measured. "My lady, we come seeking the truth. There have been troubling accusations made against you, and we wish to hear your side of the story."

The Earless' eyes narrowed, her gaze flicking between us. "Accusations? Of what nature?"

I took a deep breath, steeling myself for the conversation to come. "My lady, we have learned of assassins that seem connected to you. Tonight, they attacked your son—Ser Prenot, and me as we attended the camp outside the gates. We need to understand your role in this."

The Earless rose to her feet, shock and fear warring on her face. "My son? Assassins? Is he hurt?"

I was not expecting her to be so focused on Prenot, having already made my mind about her connection to the matter. "Uh . . . uh . . . He is hurt, my lady. Badly. A sword to the belly, he—"

Kira interrupted. "He is alive, Your Grace. He is convalescing in the camps."

"The camps? Take him immediately to the Temple . . ."

"We cannot my lady," I said. "For that is the rub. We believe that the attackers were Knights of the Tears. They wore their markings. And not a simple question of changing livery. It cannot be anything else—"

"What? You are . . ."

"My lady, I do not mean to be insensitive, but there were insinuations made in the melee. Insinuations about you. We wanted to ensure your honor was still intact, so we came directly here, knowing how such things may be interpreted," Kira stated in as deferential tone as she could muster.

The earless looked at her and then to me. She breathed a sigh of relief. "That is good that he is alive. I must see him soon. He, as you know, Ser Aaron, is my last."

"We shall make the arrangements, whatever you wish," Kira said.

But the Earless continued, "Whatever you heard in your engagement with these assassins, Ser Aaron, I assure you, I have no part in any such treachery!" I would not hurt my son."

Kira held up a hand, her voice soothing. "My lady, we do not come to judge but to understand. We only seek clarity."

The Earless hesitated, her gaze darting to the guards who still stood at attention near the door. "Ser Torren, Ser Alric, leave us. I would speak with Ser Aaron and Lady Kira alone."

The guards exchanged a glance, uncertainty written on their faces. "My lady, are you certain? We are here for your protection."

The Earless waved a hand dismissively. "I am quite capable of protecting myself, Ser Torren. Now, please, leave us."

The guards bowed and exited the room. The Earless turned back to us, her expression softening slightly. She kept her voice low. "Now, ser, what exactly was said?"

"Exactly, I am not sure I can say exactly," I thought back to that moment, the assassin jeering at us. Saying we chose against Prenot's brother . . .

"I would like to know if you can produce it from your memory, ser. I would not have this haunt me."

I remembered then. "The blackguard said, 'The Earless suffers for your failures' after he accused us of taking sides against his brother."

"Against his brother."

"Yes, against his brother. My lady, you have not been told—"

"I know, ser. I know of my son Dumont's treachery. As does the king. We have kept this silent. It would not do to have a house such as mine implicated in such a plot. But, I did not. Ser Gavreaux and the commander of Caer Gorak have both informed the king of his treachery. But—"

"You kept it quiet," Kira said.

"Yes. When they said that the Earless suffered, I can only assume that they referred to the damage done to this family's reputation or some other dark plot against me—or even the impact that losing my last son would have on me if they were to cut him down."

I had not considered this possibility. The murder of Prenot was the suffering they were referring to. A revenge for her refusal to assist Dumont in his treachery? Along with my murder and the ending of the investigation?

"My lady—" I made amends.

She cut off my foolishness and spoke. "I appreciate your willingness to hear me out, Lady Kira. As for you, Ser Aaron, I understand your protectiveness towards Ser Prenot. He is a good man, and I would never wish harm upon him."

I felt a flush of embarrassment at her words, realizing that my self-righteousness may have colored my approach. "My lady, I apologize if I have spoken out of turn. I only seek the truth."

The Earless nodded, a small smile playing at the corners of her mouth. "As do we all, Ser Aaron. The truth is that I have been working secretly to undermine the very forces that seek to bring down our king. I have long suspected the bishop of corruption, of using his position to further his own power rather than serve the will of The God."

She moved to a nearby table, shuffling through a stack of papers. "I have been gathering evidence, secretly reaching out to allies who share my concerns. But there is not much. They are very careful. To your point about the knights, ser," she looked at me. "I was afraid the Knights of Tears are trying to implicate me because they fear I will challenge in the event of the king's untimely death. But I never thought that they would be so open."

Kira took the papers, scanning them quickly. "But why not come forward sooner? Why allow the bishop's treachery to fester in the shadows?"

The Earless sighed, sinking back into her chair. "Because, Lady Kira, I am not trusted and there is not enough there. Even the king does not trust me fully. My son Dumont's actions have cast a pall over our house, and my control over a significant portion of the Crusader army makes me a threat in the eyes of many. I must tread carefully, lest I be accused of treason myself. It would be a short walk to the Breaking Star."

I felt a pang of sympathy for the Earless, realizing the precarious position she found herself in.

"My lady, I apologize for my earlier harshness. I see now the difficult path you must walk."

She waved a hand, dismissing my apology. "Think nothing of it, Ser Aaron. We are all on edge in these troubled times. But I must warn you—the bishop's reach is long, and he will stop at nothing to gain power. You must be cautious in your investigations, and trust no one fully."

Kira leaned forward, her expression earnest. "We will heed your warning, my lady. But we cannot do this alone. We need allies, resources to aid us in our fight against the bishop and his minions."

The Earless nodded, her expression thoughtful. "I will help you in any way I can, Lady Kira. But there is not much I can do."

I rose to my feet, my hand resting on the hilt of my sword. "We will not let him succeed, my lady. We will find the truth and bring those responsible to justice, no matter the cost."

The Earless smiled, a fierce light in her eyes. "I believe you will, Ser Aaron. The God has worked through you before, and seems to sit upon your shoulders, when he might abandon others. I pray he is with you both in the battles to come."

As Kira and I left the Earless' chambers, my mind raced with the implications of all we had learned. The situation was even more complex than I had initially believed. We needed allies, and we could not rely on the Earless' Crusaders and guards. She had said as much.

"We need to send word to Gavreaux," I said, my voice low and urgent. "His support could be crucial in the days ahead."

I felt a surge of determination and a renewed sense of purpose in the face of the challenges that lay ahead. As we strode through the palace halls, I sent up a silent prayer to The God, asking for strength and guidance. The fate of the Holy Kingdom, and perhaps the fate of us all, rested on the choices we were about to make. Things were rapidly coming to a head.

CHAPTER 9
GATHERING FORCES

Lady Kira and I hurried through the palace halls. Our footsteps echoed on the polished stone. The place was still dark and gloomy and the few oil lamps that burned left the hallways so dim and otherworldly that we carried a candle to help light the way. As we left the Earless Monae's chambers behind, my mind raced with the implications of all we had learned. Her revelations had cast a new light on the conspiracy, but they had also raised new questions and doubts. We had potentially eliminated a powerful enemy from our list of turncoats, but we couldn't be sure. In that regard, things had gotten murkier.

Our list of enemies was still substantial: Bishop Tooleb, Knight Commander Transom, Maester Aldric, and, of course, the Gols. And I still had no way of knowing if Renart was with us or against us. They were each powerful in their own right. Together, they would be nearly insurmountable. And our list of allies—at least ones that could help us—was thin.

Just a short walk from Lady Kira's apartments, a familiar figure emerged from the shadows, her blue eyes glinting in our meager candlelight.

My heart leaped at the sight of her. "Edweene," I whispered. Keeping my voice as level as I could, "What are you doing here?"

She moved closer, her eyes narrowed, expression grave. "Aaron, Lady Kira, you must be careful—" she began.

"Yes, Edweene, the complexity of this plot and the people involved continue to get more dangerous and more shrouded in mystery," I responded. "But, why are—"

Lady Kira placed her hand on my arm, signaling me to listen, not to talk. I, of course, complied.

"Ser, as I was saying, you must be careful now. I came to inform you that Ser Transom and the Maester Aldric are waiting for you in the Lady's apartments."

I exchanged a glance with Lady Kira, my stomach tightening with unease. "Waiting for us? Dare they enter a lady's chambers?

"It does not matter, brother," Kira said, with that practical look of hers. "We'd best be prepared for them. Thank you, Edweene, for the warning."

"Of course, my lady," Edweene smiled—as much as she ever allowed herself, anyway. "It seems I have a purpose, after all. I apologize for my reckless accusations against Lady Monae. I hope that you have proven me wrong. The young Ser Prenot deserves some respite from the horror his life has become."

"No. You were right to be concerned. But that is not the matter at hand. Why, then, have these two dangerous men come to my sister's rooms? Have they discovered our purpose?"

Edweene shook her head. "My lord do not be naïve. I am convinced if these are the conspirators—or not—they have had some inkling of your purposes since your arrival in the Holy City. I do not know their intent, but I sense danger. I no longer exist in your world, Aaron. My nature prevents it. But I watch from the shadows, and I learn much. And these men are ambitious and powerful, Aaron. They will not take kindly to your—our—meddling."

I considered her words, weighing the risks against the need for answers. "We must confront them, Lady Kira, Edweene. We cannot let them control the pace any longer. And we must get a missive through to Gavreaux as soon as we may, though I fear a message to the Stone will take days to reach him and he days to arrive here. It may be for naught."

Edweene's eyes flashed with anger. "Gavreaux? You would seek his aid, even after what he did to me?"

I sighed, running a hand through my hair. "Edweene, I know that your history with Gavreaux is complicated," I said, sighing and running a hand through my hair. But he is a man of honor, and his support could be crucial in the coming fight."

Edweene was silent for a long moment, her gaze distant. "I will never forget what he did, Aaron. But I will set aside my vengeance. For now, if you believe he can help us in this endeavor. But I do not like it. And I do not trust the man."

I placed a hand on her shoulder, feeling the tension in her muscles. "Thank you, Edweene. I know it is not easy for you."

She met my gaze, her eyes narrow and hard. "I trust you, Aaron, as always, but that does not mean that I must forget my own instincts." Then she turned to my sister. "And I trust you as well, Lady Kira. And, I do not give trust easily. I know how important a person's sister can be. And you are—"

Kira waved her hand as if brushing away Edweene's words. "Never you care, my Lady, Edweene. We are friends, you and I. That means we don't have to explain such matters to one another."

Edweene nodded. "Very well, then, if you are committed to this course of action, ser, I should tell you that Gavreaux has arrived in the Palace.

You need not worry about the time it will take him to muster his knights and come."

"That is a most unusual development. The Passage knights, in the Holy City. I wonder what the Knights of Tears think of such a thing. This has—"

"Ser," Kira broke my pontification. "The matter at hand, please."

Edweene agreed with my sister, "Yes, Aaron. The matter at hand. The enemy—at least as we now believe them to be—are waiting in your sister's apartments. Whatever shall you do?"

"Yes. Thank you for bringing me back to this. I tend to—"

"Aaron—" Kira stopped me.

"Yes. We must go there at once—"

Edweene interrupted me again. "Know this, Aaron. If Transom or Aldric threaten you or the Lady Kira, I will not hesitate to gut them both."

I nodded, a grim smile tugging at my lips. "Let us hope it does not come to that."

Together, the three of us entered Kira's apartments, steeling ourselves for the confrontation to come. Transom and Aldric stood by the window, their faces cast in shadow by the fading light. Aldric and Transom were a study in contrasts. Aldric was shorter than I, with a balding head, and a rotund belly. He wore robes of fine silk with the sign of the Star embroidered on the breast. He wore an abundance of jewelry on his wrists and fingers. A pendant of the Tear hung from an ornate chain on his neck. Transom, though not tall, had a powerful build. He wore his armor and surcoat, with the symbol of the Knights of Tears sewn into the chest, and he pinned a heavy cloak over his shoulder with a Tear-shaped broach. His beard was short, and his hair cut where it met the shoulders, in the traditional manner of the Tears. Around his waist he wore his longsword, its glittering hilt a reminder that this man was not to be trifled with. His eyes were menacing, filled with self-righteousness. My mind conjured up an image of him and I circling each other in a dance of swords where one of us would not survive.

"Ser Aaron," Transom said, his voice cold and flat. He took in my bloody armor, and disheveled look, then cast a disapproving look toward Edweene, and said, "You have been busy of late, sticking your nose where it does not belong. I am surprised you are still with us." He then added, "The God must favor you," but the tone of his voice told me it was mockery.

I stepped forward, my hand resting on the hilt of my own sword. "Indeed, it seems he does," I agreed, and saw his face twist up in a smirk. "I seek only to make truth known, Knight Commander—to shine a light on the roaches that eat away at our Holy Kingdom.

"And what is that truth, ser," he hissed and took a step toward me.

I could not help but take a step back, keeping a distance between us. But, I felt Edweene's hand on my back, as if to say, *stand firm.*

I gathered myself, and said, "That truth, my Lord, is that there is a conspiracy at work here, one that threatens the very foundations of The Crusade, The King and mocks The God and his Archbishop."

Aldric chuckled, a mirthless sound that sent a chill down my spine. "You speak of matters beyond your understanding, boy. You would do well to leave such things to your betters."

Kira spoke up then, her voice clear and strong. "And who are our betters, Maester Aldric? Those who would plot against the King and the The God, who would plunge the kingdom into chaos for their own gain?"

Transom's eyes narrowed, his hand tightening on the hilt of his weapon. "You tread dangerous ground, Lady Kira. The Knights of Tears are loyal servants of The God, and we will not tolerate such baseless accusations."

"Baseless?" I said, my anger rising. "I have seen the evidence with my own eyes, Transom. Your knights are involved in this conspiracy, and I will not rest until the truth is brought to light."

Aldric stepped forward, his face twisted with rage. "You dare to threaten us, boy? You, who are nothing more than a pawn in a game far greater than you can imagine?"

I met his gaze, refusing to be cowed. "I am no pawn, Maester Aldric. I am a knight of the Crusade, a servant of The God, and I will not be intimidated by the likes of you."

Transom and Aldric exchanged a glance, a silent communication passing between them. "This is not over, Ser Aaron," Transom said, his voice low and menacing. "We came to beseech you to turn away from your foolish and misguided quest of yours. It is heretical to speak to the bishop in this manner. But you have no concern for heresy, do you?" he cast a disapproving glance at Edweene, who I felt shift under his gaze. "You have made powerful enemies today, and you will come to regret your actions."

With that, they strode from the room, their cloaks billowing behind them. I let out a breath I hadn't realized I'd been holding, my heart pounding in my chest.

"That was a dangerous gamble, Aaron," Edweene said, her voice tight with concern.

"But a necessary one," I said. "They needed to know that we are not afraid, that we will not be silenced."

Kira placed a hand on my arm, her touch gentle but firm. "We must be careful, Aaron. They will not take this lying down."

I nodded, my mind already racing with plans and possibilities. "Kira—please attend to Gavreaux at once, asking for his aid. And then, if you may, I need you to continue your efforts here in the palace to gather what information you can about Aldric's shadowy associate. I fear he is a missing piece."

Kira smiled, a dark look in her eyes. "I will not fail you, brother."

As Kira set about her task, I turned to Edweene. "I must go to see Prenot, and tell him about his mother."

Edweene nodded, a small smile playing at the corners of her mouth. "Of course, Aaron. You're alone now, as ever. Kira must stay here, Willem must hold the troops with your man, Deres. I would be by your side again."

I felt a warmth spread through my chest at her words. It was comforting, and familiar. I belonged with her, I could not help but think, though Ser Transom's accusations of heresy burned in the back of my head, amplifying my own sense of the same. I pushed them back, and down, locking them away for the moment. I needed her with me. "Then let us go. Our duet is reunited."

Together, we left the palace and made our way to the camps. We hurried, and kept to the commonplaces, hoping to avoid an ambush. Edweene, of course, advised we take the darker, shadowy routes, but at this late hour, few would be out, and I believed the lighted thoroughfares would dissuade most would-be killers. Whatever the case, we were not molested on our trek. It was not long before we were outside the gates again and entering the large, sail-cloth tent of the camp's infirmary.

The place smelled of healing elixirs, bile, and perfumes meant to cover the smell of death. It was dark, and the tent was lit only by a few wane candles that flickered with the draft kicked up when we threw open the flap. Prenot was propped up in bed, his face pale and drawn. His eyes widened slightly at the sight of Edweene, but he quickly composed himself.

"Ser Aaron, Lady Edweene," he said, his voice weak but steady. "What news from the palace?"

I sat beside him, recounting all that had happened, from our confrontation with the Earless Monae to the tense meeting with Ser Transom and Aldric. Edweene stood above us, her presence a silent, protective thing that filled me with strange confidence. Prenot listened intently, his brow furrowed with concentration.

"The Knights of Tears . . . when you spoke of the mark on the assassin, I had my doubts. But it sounds almost unimaginable," he said, shaking his head. "I am pleased you found the truth about my mother, but I would still keep your wits about you when dealing with her. I am not convinced she was . . . no, never mind. My family has long had dealings with them, and I fear that my mother's connection to them may run deeper than we know."

I leaned forward, my elbows resting on my knees. "What do you mean, Prenot?"

He sighed, wincing slightly at the pain. "The Earless has always been ambitious, Aaron. She has always fancied herself as a kingmaker, one who could shape the destiny of the Holy Kingdom. And the Knights of Tears, with their power and influence, would make powerful allies in such a quest."

Edweene spoke up then, her voice low and thoughtful. "The Earless is a formidable woman, and her ambitions are not to be underestimated. But we must be careful not to let suspicion cloud our judgment. I was first to accuse her, ser, but as I watched the exchange from the shadows, I must say, she seemed to be true. The true enemy here is the bishop and those who align with him."

I nodded, considering her words. "You're right, Edweene. We must focus on the task at hand and not let ourselves be distracted by the machinations of others. Let us have faith in your blood, ser, your brother notwithstanding. The Earless has as much to gain by being the King's protector."

Prenot struggled to sit up straighter, his face tight with pain. "Whatever the Earless' role in this, I know I must do my part to help. I may be wounded, but my mind is sharp, and I have knowledge that could be of use." His desperation to take part despite his foul wound was perhaps admirable, but disconcerting all the same.

I placed a hand on his shoulder, settling him back against the pillows. "Rest now, Prenot. We will come to you if needs be."

As Edweene and I left the infirmary, I felt a renewed sense of purpose, a clarity of focus. I attribute that to Edweene. When we are apart, things are simply not as clear. I turned to Edweene, meeting her gaze with a smile. "Thank you for being here, Edweene. Things . . . things are more difficult without you."

She returned my smile, her blue eyes softening. "That is pleasing, Aaron. We are in this together, come what may," she said.

As we made our way back through the palace halls, I felt a sense of hope. The road ahead was ever more perilous, and we had lost a powerful sword arm in Prenot. But I could not help thinking that Edweene and I would solve this thing together. In the end, I hoped it was not the power of kings or bishops that would decide the fate of the Holy Kingdom but the courage and determination of those who fought for what was right. If not, our mission was doomed.

CHAPTER 10
THE BISHOP'S GAMBIT

I jolted awake and gasped. My heart pounded against my ribcage, and the remnants of a familiar nightmare still clung to my mind. The image of Edweene's piercing blue eyes as I drove my dagger through her heart seared into my thoughts. As my vision cleared, I stared into those very same eyes.

Edweene stood over me, staring at me, her foot nudging my side insistently. "Wake up, Aaron," she said, her voice cutting through the early morning stillness. "I have a message from Kira."

I sat up and shook the sleep out of my head, and disbursed the dream. The rough blanket fell away from my body as I rubbed the sleep from my eyes. The cool, damp air of the tent sent a shiver down my spine, and I could feel the weight of Edweene's gaze upon me. "What is it?" I asked, my voice still raspy from sleep.

"The bishop has made his move," Edweene said. Her words hung in the air like a threat. "He's accused the Earless Monae of treason and demanded the King arrest her. According to Kira, the bishop made the announcement in front of the court, with every noble person of import in the Holy Land present—at least those in Clurak this day."

The words hit me like a physical blow, and I felt my blood turn to ice in my veins. Clearly, she exaggerated. Not all the noble families were in the Holy City, but many of them were. And many of them regularly attended the bishop's and the King's joint sessions. "What? How could he do that?" I asked as though she had an answer. I struggled to get my head mind around what could have precipitated such a move, and what evidence they would need to present. Regardless of the implications of this news.

Edweene shook her head, her hair falling across her face like a shadow. "The court is in an uproar. The news hasn't spread widely yet, but it's only a matter of time before the entire city is buzzing with the scandal."

"What—What did they present?" I asked. I stood up, my bare feet pressing against the earth as I paced the small confines of the tent. The musty smell of canvas and sweat, the rocky ground poking through the thin ground cloth, and the frosty morning air all faded to nothing as my mind was consumed with the weight of the situation.

"Nothing, I am told, ser," she answered. "The bishop said that he would present something this evening to the King and his advisors. Transom and Gavreaux are apparently among them, as is the Maester."

"This must be a diversion," I said, as I worked through all the scenarios I could fathom. "A way to draw attention away from his own treachery. Perhaps our confrontation drove this. An attempt to get ahead of us. Or . . ."

"Or perhaps this is the beginning of the coup. Setting up the Earless for the eventual murder. The evidence presented before the fact." She said.

"I think you are right, my lady," I looked at those striking azure pools that carried so much of my past in weighty dreams and reminders of my guilt. I couldn't look away from her. Perhaps by finding some semblance of justice in this and stopping this terrible thing, I could relieve some of that pain—some of my guilt. I said, "After this, it will be difficult for her to deny."

I pulled my eyes away and began to dress.

That's what I suspect as well," Edweene agreed, her eyes tracking my movements like a hawk. "But the damage is done. The Earless is in grave danger, and we must make haste if we hope to save her."

I faced Edweene as I slid my mail shirt over my head. My eyes locked on hers again, and at that moment, I saw a flicker of something in her gaze, a mix of concern and emotion that I rarely see in the eyes of the lych. It was disconcerting, to say the least. I tried to give her a nonchalant grin. "Do not worry, lych," I said jokingly. We shall survive as we always do."

"I am not concerned for me, Aaron. I am already gone. My soul has long since been forsaken." She waved her ring—the phylactery that held her soul—in front of my face. "I worry about you . . . and your sister, of course."

"Of course," I mimicked. "And the Crusade?" I asked.

"I do not care for these Holy Fools. I care for you, Aaron. You are my only—"

"Edweene," I said . . . I reached out and pulled her in. She did not feel cold, as a forsaken soul should. She never had. And I suddenly wondered if her soul was truly lost. Or if that was some misapplication, or misinterpretation of the word of The God. She pushed me away as soon as I pressed against her.

"Enough, Aaron. You mock me. I am not to be held like a child."

My heart dropped. I meant not to mock her or make light of her concern. I meant to comfort her. I continue to make a fool of myself when it comes to her.

"We will be fine." I said, my voice filled with a sudden sense of purpose. "Me and my sister—and you too," I smiled. She did not smile back. I continued, "We need something to expose the bishop's true intentions and clear the Earless' name."

Edweene nodded, a sly smile playing at the corners of her mouth. "I can try to help with that," she said, her voice low and conspiratorial. "I will try to spy on the bishop's inner circle, gather information from the inside. I am sure they will be aflutter with activity today."

I felt a surge of fear at the thought of Edweene putting herself in danger. I reached out instinctively, my hand grasping her arm. She pulled away from me. "No, it's too risky," I said, my voice filled with concern. "If you are discovered—"

Edweene placed her hand over mine, her fingers curling around my wrist in a gesture of reassurance. With unnatural strength, she peeled my hand away. "Aaron, this is what I am going to do. This is not your choice," she said, her voice soft but firm.

I sighed, knowing well that I could not dissuade her. "Very well," I said, my voice heavy with resignation. "But be careful, Edweene. I can't—"

She smiled then, a rare softness in her eyes. "You won't fool," she said. With that, she slipped out of the tent, disappearing into the dawn like a ghost.

I finished dressing quickly, strapped on my sword, and stepped out of the tent. The cool morning air hit me like a slap in the face. I breathed deeply. All around me, the Crusade was waking up. The smell of cook fires and coffee, the sound of mail and horses, the cries of sergeants and men as they were called out of their tents and bunks to training or whatever activity might await them. Soon, the Crusade would hear about the bishop's proclamation. Tens of thousands of holy warriors were called by the archbishop and the King. If I could not stop this, they would be put to terrible use, and the holy war would start again in earnest. The Crusaders were ready for it. Indeed, many were seeking to find the archbishop's absolution and bring steel to the Gol.

I took a deep breath, pushed all those concerns I could not control from my mind, and steeled myself for the task ahead.

The streets of the city were already beginning to stir as I made my way back towards the palace, the sound of merchants hawking their wares and the clatter of hooves on cobblestones filling the air. But beneath the usual bustle of city life, I knew things were quickly coming to a head—whether the potters, thatchers, blacksmiths, beggars, and carpenters did or not. News of the Earless Monae's impending arrest had begun spreading. Small groups of people gathered on street corners, their heads bent together in whispered conversation. As I passed, I caught snatches of their words, fears, and rumors mingling together in a cacophony of unease.

"Did you hear? The Earless Monae, a traitor to the crown!"

"I always knew there was something off about her."

"Impossible. The Earless is true to the God. I don't believe it."

"But why would the bishop accuse her? Surely he must have evidence?"

The God was speaking to them in their hearts, and such energy was commutable. Clurak would be on fire soon. A growing tension and crackle of unease, if only imagined, set my nerves on edge. I gritted my teeth and pressed on.

The palace guards eyed me warily as I passed, their hands gripping their polearms. I imagined the entire city was holding its breath, waiting for the storm to break. Kira was waiting for me in her chambers, her face drawn with worry as she paced the room. She rushed to me when I entered and pulled me into the room, slamming the door behind. "Aaron, thank The God you're here," she said, her voice strained with emotion. "The bishop will announce his accusations tonight at court. He painted the Earless as a traitor to the crown during the audience this morning, and some self-serving nobles and knights are believing him. It is not just those who hold land in the Holy Kingdom, but Crusaders as well."

I shook my head, anger rising in my chest like a fire. "We will not let this stand, Kira," I said, my voice filled with determination. "We have to clear her name, to expose the bishop's lies for what they are." But we have little or nothing to go on. We had Prenot, who had knowingly ignored the King's orders. We had the Earless, whose son had betrayed the crown and the Crusade. And we had me, a man who was never much liked by my peers—a knight made a hero by circumstance. There was no evidence to speak of. Nothing we could hand over to the King to deny the charges—whatever they might be. The evening audience had to be stopped.

Kira nodded; her jaw was set. "I've been reaching out to our allies, gathering support where I can. But we need more than just words, Aaron. We need evidence, something concrete that we can use against the bishop."

"Edweene is working on that," I said. I kept my voice low instinctively, though there was likely no one around to hear. "She's gone to spy on the bishop's inner circle, likely watching from the shadows. If anyone can uncover the truth, it's her."

Kira's eyes widened, and I could see the fear that flickered behind them. "That's a dangerous game she's playing, Aaron," she said, her voice filled with concern. "If she's discovered—"

"Did you meet with Gavreaux?" I asked quickly, meaning to divert the conversation from where my heart was already worried.

"Yes, as you asked."

"And what came of it?"

"I'm sorry. I forgot to say in my panic. He knows we are right. He understands the risks. But he needs evidence to move. Outside the town—north on the Pilgrim's Approach—his knights are camped—a thousand or more. But they will not move without orders."

"Okay. But they are here," I said, my own fears weighing heavily on my mind. "They are our best chance. We have to trust in her abilities, in her strength."

"So, what do we do now, Aaron?"

"I suppose we wait," I said.

She nodded, and said, "I cannot. I must do something."

"Lady, there is naught we can do."

"Perhaps, Aaron. I agree with one thing: you must wait here then. For Edweene to return. That is necessary. And I shall go see the Earless."

"You cannot. For all we know, the enemy will have an ambush waiting, looking for would-be conspirators. And she has made known that she won't support us without ironclad evidence. Should we not do the same?"

"This is a fool's notion, Aaron. And self-serving. She needs companionship. This is an opportunity to build bonds with a powerful noble—"

"Kira . . . the woman has her retainers and loyal banners surrounding her. She has more friends at court than you or I and she is quite capable of looking after herself."

"You know nothing of court and the stickiness of loyalty within these walls, Aaron. I am sure that even now, everyone distances themselves from her. I am going. This gesture will prove itself valuable in the end."

I could see I had no choice in the matter. Her mind was set. "Fine," I said. "I shall go—"

"No, Aaron. You must wait for Edweene. She counts on you, as does the Crusade and the king, whether or not he knows it. This endeavor is in your hands, Aaron. It is your burden. I only mean to provide comfort to our only ally in the palace."

Kira slipped out the door and closed it shut behind her, leaving me alone in her chambers. Resolved to wait, but feeling uncomfortable and useless, I sat at her table and peered into the mirror. A man stared back at me, and I did not immediately recognize him. Who had I become? I was so far from that Dark Man who had driven his dagger into the Nun's heart. And yet, she haunted me, those eyes filled with gratitude, and conviction. She had told me time and again that I had saved her, but my heart always told me the opposite.

I let my fingers touch the mirrored glass and some part of me wished I had met Edweene long before the Gol had captured her, long before I had answered the Clarion call of the archbishop. Maybe—

I was brought from my musings by the door slamming open. I leaped up and drew my steel, ready to face anything that came. But, it was not a fight I saw, but a horror that I'd feared since Edweene had left that morning. Edweene practically fell into Kira's chambers, her lithe form battered and bleeding from a missile that protruded from her side.

My heart nearly exploded, and I caught my breath. "Edweene! What happened?" I rushed to catch her as she crumpled.

Her piercing blue eyes burned with intensity. "The bishop . . . he proclaimed she has fled after being implicated in a conspiracy to assassinate the King and betray the realm to the Gols."

"I do not care about that," I hissed at her, as I held her in my arms. All that mattered right then was the lych whose blood leaked over my arms. I kicked the door shut and pulled her to the bed.

"You must," she said.

"But—"

"Aaron. You know I will survive this. I still wear the ring. You must listen." Her breath was short, labored.

I swallowed my pain, my fear. "Okay, Edweene," I choked out. "But where is she? What proof will he offer? Kira has left for the Earless' chambers as we speak. And now, I worry for her."

"None yet," Edweene gritted out. "But Renart carries orders for the Bishop's Tears—his personal retinue—to strike down the Lord Commander Gaveaux, and deal with the Earless' Treason immediately. She is to be brought to the palace."

My stomach turned over. "Treason," I whispered rhetorically. We'd known it was being planned, but now that things were in motion, it seemed madness.

"False evidence is being fabricated. Yes, treason against the king and the Crusade, and heresy against The God." Edweene continued grimly. "Documents, paid witnesses, all portraying her actions as part of a treacherous plot to aid the Gols. All a ruse to cover the bishop's own naked ambition to seize power. And they have us . . . well, you and me. They know what I am. They bring that to the King. And they place the Earless as complicit in Dumont's treachery. The framework is being laid now. But first is the Earless."

"Edweene, we'd best get Lady Kira and leave—"

Edweene's bloodied fingers grasped at my tunic urgently. "No . . . a few moments more. At the heart of it all . . . the Earless is already being held by the Bishop's Tears. Her absence . . . not of her own making . . . they would have the King think it is. If we don't retrieve her quickly . . ."

"We have got to find Renart, and get that missive," I said. "But first, we've got to get my sister and get out of here."

"I know where he is," she said and slipped into the quiet reverie of a lych that needed to feed.

CHAPTER 11
THE EARLESS

My heart raced as I cradled Edweene's wounded form, her life's essence slowly seeping out. She fought to stay conscious, her piercing blue eyes flickering.

"Aaron . . . Renart's location. . . you must . . ." Her words became faint and slurred. Visions of the night we'd taken Dumont's soul rushed around me, consuming me in a racing heart and rapid breaths. *Not again. Not again.*

Before I could respond, the chamber door burst open. Kira rushed in. Her eyes were wide with panic. Close on her heels stomped two of the king's guards, spears leveled menacingly.

"Step away from the witch, ser!" One of them barked. "She is to be taken into custody by order of His Grace, the Bishop!"

I instinctively placed my body between them and the fallen Edweene. Already, her eyes had slipped shut, her shallow breaths the only sign she still clung to life.

Kira moved to my side, pleading with the intruders. "This is madness! She's badly wounded. She needs a hospitaller's care!"

"She needs a purifying fire is what she needs," the second guard spat, sneering at Edweene's seemingly lifeless husk. "Now stand aside, lest you be seen as conspirators against the King and Holy Church yourselves!"

My hand tightened around my sword hilt as resolve solidified in my chest. Over Edweene's prone body, I met the guards' hateful gaze with undisguised contempt.

"You are King's Men. You don't know what your meddling will do here. Touch her, and you'll get fewer courtesies than you've shown," I stated flatly. "The bishop has overstepped his bounds with his treachery. The Lady Edweene is under my protection—by the grace of the King himself, regardless of any lies that churlish snake may have invented to get you to chase my sister like dogs. For whom do you work, men, the king or the bishop?"

My bravado was a desperate gambit but one I hoped would buy us a few crucial moments. Edweene's labored breathing had already become more strained. I couldn't let her slip away before I learned where Renart could be found—her information was now life or death for the Earless.

The guards wavered, conflict and uncertainty playing out on their faces. Despite my brave front, I knew it was only a matter of time before more of their kind arrived. Or worse, the Bishop's Tears themselves.

"Quickly, while we have a moment's pause," I hissed at Kira. "Help me get her onto the bed, and let's see if we can rouse her senses once more."

Nodding grimly, my sister slipped past the confused guards to Edweene's other side. Together, we lifted the fallen lych onto the small bed, laying her out as gently as we could manage. All the while, I kept one eye trained balefully on our would-be jailers.

"Come on, Edweene," I murmured under my breath. "Fight, damn you. Your secrets could be all that saves the Earless from the bishop's depravity!"

Leaning in close, I pressed my ear near her blue-tinged lips, desperate to catch any whispery murmurings that could lead us to the wretched Renart and the key to the bishop's plot. Kira grasped Edweene's limp hand, staring at me imploringly.

Just when it seemed like the lych might have lapsed fully into unconsciousness, those chilling azure eyes flickered open once more. Her gaze met mine, and I saw not only determination and hunger, but her lych's hunger. I'd seen it before. I pushed Kira away.

"Stand away, Lady," I said, trying to be as polite as possible as I managed the situation. If Edweene had contacted her skin, the result could have been horrific.

Edweene flashed me a thankful smile as Kira cast me a nasty stare.

"Behind . . . the Temple . . ." Edweene rasped with obvious effort. "In the outbuildings . . . Renart skulks and waits for word . . ."

It was all I needed. I pulled a pillow covering the bed and quickly staunched her wound, careful not to touch her skin in this state while she was not sufficiently awake to allay her consuming nature. I whispered gruffly in her ear. "Rest now, Edweene. You've given us what we require. Kira and I will take it from here and see the Earless freed. I swear this on whatever scrap of honor I have left in me."

Straightening, I turned to face the guards again, my expression a mask of brooding thunder.

"On your way, men. The king would not have you do this. When these matters are resolved, you shall find gratitude from your king that you let us leave tonight. You know this. I know you do. The bishop's scheme has hit its first of many snags on this night. If you value your wretched lives, I suggest avoiding further entanglement."

Thankfully, they required no more convincing. They looked at one another and grimaced. The lead sergeant, who had so aggressively called Edweene a witch earlier, spoke, his voice low and conspiratorial, "You'd best be gone, ser . . . and you, Lady Kira as well. Take the abomination with you. The bishop has the run of the place this day, and he has made it known she is a sacrilege, a witch, and you are with her. You must go quickly, for more will come. And these will wear the coat of the Tears, I am sure."

Edweene lay motionless, having spent the last of her ebbing vitality. But she had accomplished what she set out to do. Now it was our turn to see her sacrifice made meaningful.

With a sharp nod to my sister, I led the way past the two guards and into the night. Between us, we carried Edweene, her silent form barely strong enough to keep her arms about our shoulders.

We left the palace behind and slid into the shadowed back alleys and service roads of Clurak. The battle for the soul of the Holy Land had begun in earnest. We would find Renart's bolt hole behind the Temple. And whether through his forced confession or the bishop's other sins exposed, the Earless would breathe free air again before this night's end.

A grim look passed between Edweene and my sister as I caught Kira up on events. "The bishop has already taken her into custody using his personal guards, the Bishop's Tears. It is a secret, meant to make it look like she is escaping the king's justice. If we don't act swiftly, he means to make a public spectacle of her ..."

The Bishop's Tears were elite, zealous knights recruited from the ranks of the Knights of Tears, and likely meant that the bishop was personally involved. I doubted that he'd allow Aldric to command his private retinue. The thought of the woman being used as a pawn in the bishop's grotesque theater had my rage burning like an ember ready to burst into flame, and it took great effort to keep it controlled. "Edweene says that Renart is near the Temple," I said. There are only a few places down there in which he could hide. I doubt the Knights of Tears would allow him entrance, at least to their sanctum. They are very secretive. That meant he was probably in the oratory or scriptorium. The oratory was the more likely, as disturbing the scribes was tantamount to sacrilege. But maybe that was the point.

"We start with the Oratory," I said, doing my best to keep the desperation and anger out of my tone. "Then, if we do not find him there, we go to the scriptorium. After that, if the man is not in my hands, I am busting into the temple itself," I swore.

"Aaron," Kira said, "Perhaps I should put Willem on notice, and you can do what you must. I will provide no benefit to your swordplay."

"That is a good idea. I am a fool for not thinking about it first," I said.

"Your mind is occupied with thoughts of the one you—"

"Do not say it, please," I said. I did not need this moment to be reminded of my unnatural feelings for Edweene.

The lych cast me a baleful look and smiled thinly. "Always . . . the godly man," she rasped out.

Why am I like this? I hurt her with every word I spoke. I squeezed her hand, grateful for her forgiveness. *Who is it here who has no soul, the Lych or the knight of the Crusade?*

It was not long before we'd made it out of the palace grounds, out of Hightown, and into the Temple district. Here, the Mount of Tears rose before us; the golden dome of the Temple of Tears rose like a beacon to The God himself. The road here turned from bumpy, unimproved cobble to flattened, smooth stone that led straight for the stairs that took pilgrims to the Holiest site on Korannah. A feeling of awe settled upon me, and I felt my sins more poignantly than just five steps before, as though the dome magnified them with its majesty. I had stood in the shadow of that dome before, and every time I experienced it, the same feeling of insignificance settled upon me. It gave me confidence that our mission was true, that The God did indeed live here, and we were his servants.

But today was not the time for contemplation. Much of that would come later. I made the sign of the Star in respect. How I desired to look upon the Star and experience its grandeur. There was a way into the temple beneath the mount upon which it stood. I'd used it to enter long days past while doing the work of the Dark Men. I briefly considered the idea of entering and seeking Transom or the bishop within. *Could I end this all so easily with a sword to the Commander's neck?* I dismissed it. I could not guarantee that I would find him or have the evidence to free us all from evil accusations. So, I dismissed the idea. No, our path did not take us there, and for that, I felt a small amount of disappointment.

It would have to wait. We turned from the principal thoroughfare—the path the God had taken on his way to martyrdom, now paved and polished to a sheen that glittered like silver and bronze—and slipped into the Circle Road. The Circle Road gave entry to all the Temple outbuildings, chapels, vendor warehouses, and even billeting for the Knights of Tears. The first building we came to was the oratory, where I had divined our quarry and was likely waiting to meet with some dark and corrupt agent of the Tears.

I led them into a short alley across the street, and we placed Edweene on the ground, positioning her back against the wall of a warehouse across from the oratory, ensuring that she could not be easily seen.

He's here. I felt it. The God was leading me here. I felt it, in my heart.

"I'd best be gone," Kira said to me. "Off to the camp."

"You'd best," I agreed. "I worry about you. Be careful, sister, and stick to the dark places where the agents of the traitor cannot find you."

"Aaron, have you not learned? You worry too much. I am quite the spy."

She was correct. "Please, allow me my delusions. I care for you and would have you be safe. The God is with you, Kira. I know it."

"And with you, Aaron. He is with us all." She looked down at Edweene, who rested now, pale and—if such a thing could be—near death. "And with your lych, Aaron. He is with her, too. I believe it," she said.

And I, if truth be told, believed it too. I kneeled next to her. "Edweene. I am sorry. I will bring you back. And I am here with you, even if I am not by your side. Your soul is mine," I said. I leaned over, and, with great trepidation, I placed my lips upon her head and kissed her gently. It felt cold, and something passed through me. I felt a small tug deep inside me, as though someone was pulling a string attached to my heart. I gasped and planted my hands against the wall as I felt myself slipping away, my mind going blank for a startling moment. Kira's hands gripped my shoulders and pulled me away.

Edweene's blue eyes fluttered open. She gazed into mine and said nothing for a long, frightening moment as the tugging abated. "Thank you," she said. I did not take much—only enough to watch. I hope you do not mind."

I realized then that she had drawn from me. Strength, Spirit, Soul? I knew not what it was, but I was happy to give it. I nodded to her. "I must go in now," I said. "And Kira must leave. Will you be all right?"

"I will," she affirmed.

And Kira patted her hand and left, slipping between buildings in her brocaded gown as she went. I nodded a goodbye to Edweene and jogged across the road to the side of the oratory. The building was strangely shaped, a large central chapel surrounded by and connected to several small buildings for private worship. Like everything built to honor The God, it was laid out in the shape of a five-pointed star on a central hub, its topmost point facing the Temple of Tears. Glittering stained glass windows looked out from the outbuildings upon the Circle Road and gave those within—at least in the three pods that could see it—a spectacular view of the Golden Dome of Tears.

He would be in one of the rear two oratories, not one so easily seen by potential enemies. I hoped that my instincts were right, that The God led me true. I was not sure there was time to make my way to the Scriptorium. The knights would be coming for their directions soon enough. It must be this. It must be.

I circled behind, and before long, I was out one of the back two buildings. I peered through the stained glass. All within was shaded in orange and blue, and distorted from the thick glass. But there was nothing there. The chamber was empty. I ducked down and went to the other. Here, I had more luck.

I thanked The God, for when I looked in, I saw him. Renart, or so I presumed, dressed in his dark robes. His hood was down, but his back was to me. I glimpsed his face as he looked about the room. Indeed, I'd been right. The God had led me true. It was Renart. He faced the front door that led to the central chapel. He was waiting for someone. The man gripped something in his hand. I lowered my head below the sill and crouch-walked to the covered causeway between.

I slid along the wall, and reached the door. I pushed it open. When I entered, Renart nearly jumped out of his skin.

"Well, well, well," I growled, stalking forward to glare down into his eyes. "If it isn't the most vile serpent in the bishop's nest of vipers."

He stepped back and threw off his cloak. He drew his sword, and leveled the point toward me. "Be gone, ser," he said. This is no place for you. "If you leave, you have not committed treason."

I slid my own steel from its scabbard and stepped into the chamber. "I'd rather not kill you so close under the eyes of God," I implored him and made the sign of the Star on my chest. "Roll your bones right, Renart, and you will still be on the right side of this thing. Hand me whatever you have there in your hand."

"I cannot, ser," he said. "The Tears will be here soon. I don't even know what is in this letter."

"So, we shall do this the hard way. You should know I slew Rayfe the Darkstalker. I killed the Tawl and threw down Ek Inir Ahn, the great Gol General. I've made short work of much better than the likes of you."

"I have no choice, my lord," he eked out. "It was all the Earless' doing, she's in league with the Gol savages, I swear!"

I leaned in quickly, my sword a flash. It slipped past his awkward, unprepared guard and cut a ribbon across his upper arm. He dropped his sword and stepped back against the altar. He slid the scroll case into his belt and fumbled with his dagger.

I did not allow him time to do so. I rushed forward and backhanded the man across his mouth with the pommel of my sword. His teeth gave way, and his cheekbone cracked beneath the strike.

I sneered with disgust as he let loose his knife, dropping it to the ground.

"Keep weaving those lies, and you'll taste the blade next time. The bishop is at the heart of this conspiracy. You and I both know it."

"No, I fear he speaks the truth insofar as he knows it," Edweene's faint voice cut through the tension like a knife's edge. I turned to see her standing in the door. She was hunched over, gripping her wounded side. Eyes glittering, she whispered to me, with great strain, "It seems your soul is stronger than you give it credit for."

I did not ask how she could sense someone's duplicitousness. The answer would likely upset me more. "Edweene, please. You are not well—"

Her eyes flashed to Renart. "Tell them what you know about the Earless' location, worm. Tell them . . . or I'll show you what terror true oblivion tastes like . . ." She twisted the words like she meant them. But I could tell she was struggling to even stay standing. Blood seeped through her fingers, and she leaned against the doorjamb.

Renart froze, his eyes bugging out as some unseen horror seemed to snake through his mind's eye. Twisting under Edweene's horrifying gaze, he began to keen softly.

"Edweene, this is not the way . . ."

"We . . . have . . . no . . . time, ser," she said. "The coup is upon us, and this man is our only hope."

And suddenly, the words started tumbling from his cracked lips. The Bishop has her imprisoned in a secret cell under the Temple of Tears itself! Guarded by the Knights of Tears—the Bishop's Tears, his personal huscarls. He . . ." Whatever was happening behind Renart's bulging eyes—whatever dark visions Edweene was projecting into him—doubled him over retching. He recovered. "He plans to keep her hidden 'till she confesses. Then . . ."

Without warning, he made a dash for the door—a fool's move. He took two steps before my sword found his abdomen. He fell forward, sliding across my blade. I yanked it free as he fell to his knees at my feet, grasping his ruined gut, gurgling, and begging for help.

"How do we know he's telling the truth?" I asked. I knit my brow with skepticism.

"Oh, he's telling the truth," Edweene murmured, never unlocking her gaze from Renart's, even as he struggled to stay up.

"You're drying, my friend," I said. I felt the coldness that I'd been hiding since I left the Dark Men take me. "It's time to make things right with The God before you expire. Tell us all you know. We'll find out, anyway. The Temple is just up the hill."

From somewhere, he found some semblance of strength. He pulled his eyes from Edweene and spat at me. I flinched as blood and spittle dotted my face.

"Your bed is made, then."

"So be it, ser. At least I do not cavort with demons."

"Oh, Renart," I said, having suddenly come to grips with where things stood. "You'll do more than cavort with her . . ." I pushed him back against the altar. He hissed at me, breathing hard, blood bubbling through his lips and leaking through his fingers.

"You're fading, Edweene," I said, voice tight as I looked up at her and took in her increasingly haggard appearance. "Forcing the truth from Renart's took all that was left, didn't it?"

She opened her mouth to protest, "Aaron, I know how this makes you—"

I silenced her with a look and a gentle touch to her pale cheek. "I would have you alive for the endgame, Edweene."

Pulling close, I could feel the weary aura washing off her diminutive frame in soul-weary waves. My voice dropped to a throaty murmur. "I know what I must do. What you need of me. Take your strength, Edweene . . . and be whole again."

With that terrible benediction, I guided her hand to Renart's lank, matted hair and pressed her fingers down over his scalp. His eyes shot wide, and he gasped. "No . . . by The God, no!"

I closed my ears to him. Ignoring his pleas and repeating God's mantra repeatedly in my mind as though I could cleanse the taint of what we were doing here away.

"Edweene's eyelids fluttered, her beautiful face slackened as her thrall took hold. Slowly, inexorably, she began to feed—her unspeakable hunger sated through violating the deepest sanctity of Renart's very essence. I watched in mingled rapture and revulsion until the wretched spy went limp and desiccated on the floor.

When her eyes fluttered open, I could once again see the baneful vitality emanating from the deep azure glow. Whatever unclean hunger possessed her was gone, and her strength quickly returned. She eyed me as she breathed deeply. Whatever re-invigoration energy flowed into her, and her eyes softened. She gave a single sedate nod of thanks as she recovered.

I returned the nod brusquely, struggling to maintain my composure. I had known the day would come when I would have to witness Edweene's . . . condition again. And it tore at me. But for the Earless' life, for the sanctity of the realm itself—for Edweene's life, there was no line I would not cross.

Edweene and I exchanged a dark look—time was disappearing quickly. We had to penetrate the bishop's sanctum and free the Earless before a catastrophe befell all of The Crusade and the Holy Land.

"Let us go," I said to Edweene. "Let us plumb the heresy from the heart of the Temple of The Tears.

Chapter 12

Beneath the Golden Dome

The grim silence that followed Edweene's grotesque ritual filled the air, suffocating us with its weight. My gaze remained fixed on Renart's lifeless husk even as Edweene straightened, her preternatural vitality renewed through that most profane of violations.

She stepped over the remains, her piercing eyes locking mine as she breathed deeply and stumbled against the wall, still recovering from the feeding. For a mortifying instant, all I could see was the depths of unholy hunger that lurked behind that azure gaze. I closed my eyes and pushed it out of my mind. It was enough that she was back, alive.

"I am sorry, ser knight," she heaved out, her voice concerned and broken by the traumatic event. Her downcast eyes revealed shame and embarrassment, as if caught doing something unconscionable. "I know that was hard for you. It is hard for me too. It is how I must survive sometimes. It is how I heal—"

"I know, Edweene. You must not apologize. I understand. We are who—and what—we are. You did not choose this. And I . . . I have taken part in it. If it is unforgivable sin, then I am as lost as you. But I cannot—will not—believe it. The God still favors us. And I need you. There is no time for self-flagellation and recrimination." Even as I said it, I wondered if I believed my own words. But I knew I must for my life, and all that I had done, to make sense. "Renart was a wicked man . . . perhaps the worst—a man whose allegiances changed more often than his clothing. We can trust the bishop more than we can trust the likes of him. At least the bishop pursues his own agenda and does not play at pursuing another. The world is better without him." I said these things as much for me as for her. Justification for a depraved act, that I could not even understand. What sustained her? The flesh or the spirit? Are they the same? "The Crusade and the Holy Land needs you . . ."

She peered at me, eyes narrowed and expectant, and pushed herself from the wall. "I need you, Aaron." She gestured back and forth between her and me. "I need this. If even a friendship. It is the only meaning—"

"Let us get on with this, then, my friend. Let us do what we have come for. Are you up for it? Recovered enough to move."

"Yes, ser. The Earless needs us."

"You're right . . . of course you are. Gather what you need from our fallen friend, and let's see this through. No more . . . indulgences." My gaze fell hard upon her once more. "Not until this conspiracy lies gutted, at least."

The words sounded hollow even to my ears, a desperate attempt to reassert some semblance of control over the rapidly fracturing situation. Edweene's brow arched, her expression an unreadable mask as she knelt beside Renart's remains.

With deft motions, she rifled his pockets and robes for anything useful, including the sealed scroll case. As she held the ornate tube gently, she rolled it over in her hands, feeling the intricate carvings beneath her fingertips. "This is partially what we came for, is it not?" With a gentle gesture, she offered it to me, her hand outstretched. "We should make haste," she continued, voice taut and urgent. "Whatever profanities lurk within this scroll, they may unlock the path to the Earless . . . and spell the bishop's damnation."

I took the scroll case, weighing it in my hands. It was heavy to me—at least in its import. The tube may have been but a small piece of carved wood, but inside could be the evidence that would bring down the conspiracy. It was a leaden cloak.

"You're right," I replied with a heavy sigh. "Still, we dare not break this seal until presenting it before the King himself. If the bishop's treacheries are truly inside, the seal's integrity must remain inviolate as evidence."

I tucked the scroll case securely away as we prepared to brave the Temple's unholy depths. My heart soared at the thought of the incendiary contents that could be within those sealed edges. If we could bring them to the king—

"Are you prepared to free the Earless, now?" she asked, a chipper tune to her voice.

I laughed at her attempt to insert levity in her tone. But it was not genuine. I fell silent for a beat, steeling my nerves. *Was I prepared?*

"Of course," I grunted at last. "For the King. For the Earless. For the God himself if I must. Let us free her now and return a mother to her son and secure a kingdom for a king." It sounded foolish and light. But it felt right to me, just then. We were here for the right reasons, even if the ghastly act we'd just committed on The God's sacred ground seemed to undermine its rightness.

Edweene's lips quirked ever so slightly at that, a wintry half-smile of what could've been pride or mockery—even mirth. Or perhaps a bit of all those things. "Then let's be about it, Ser Aaron. First, we kill those who hold her and break her

bonds. Then we can sweat over the Temple poli-
tics . . ."

Falling into grim silence, we slipped out of the
oratory and back into the shadowed alley behind the abbey-like structure. It was midday now,
and the evening was rapidly approaching. The
king held his audience at nightfall, so we had
little time. Edweene was still recovering, and her
wounded lope forced our pace to little more than
a shuffle. But we could not wait for her to fully
recover. Time was our sworn enemy.

As we neared the imposing footprint of the
Temple itself, Edweene suddenly froze mid-step.
I halted beside her, opening my mouth to in-
quire, when I saw her nostrils flare and those delicate features contort into a mask of revulsion.
"Corpse fires . . ." she whispered grimly, and I
flinched at the start of the sacrilegious curse. ". .
. and with burned offerings to fuel them. How do
we get inside, Aaron?"

"I know a way. It is a route that I used when
I walked a darker path, and we wished for our
methods to be kept from prying eyes."

"You mean hidden from the light of day," she countered.

I could not disagree. "The same," I said.

We skirted around and away from the main thoroughfare, sidestepping deeper into the shadows between the ancillary chapels and shrines. All the while, the visions of days gone assaulted me with memories best left forgotten. It had been years since I had taken part in the methods of the Dark Men, but those days were clear to me, as if yesterday. The horrors that the Temple's masters had already set in motion seemed like an extension of those days to me, and I was convinced that it was time to put it behind me—and to deliver this holy place from the darkness that now ruled there.

I led us to the rear of the temple. We were hurrying, as the Mount is not small, and circling its base was no easy feat in the time we had. We arrived at a side avenue on Circle Road and followed it to the left. By this time, Edweene had recovered her strength and agility, and moved once again like the shadow she'd become. She crept ahead of me as the avenue continued through the last few ante-buildings on the Circle before it cut into the Mount. Earthen rises on either side of its cobbled path soon loomed over us. We inched along the edge of the path until we reached a chest-high iron fence and gate, where we crouched. A small stone structure built into the mount stood across from us, its heavy stone door engraved with the Tear of The God. A singular guard waited outside, wearing the livery of the Knights of Tears. He paced back and forth, inattentive to matters at hand.

"There," I whispered. "Inside there, we will find a passage that will take us to the tombs of the priests, vestals, and knights. Among the dead, there is a secret way into the Tears. I used it often . . . in a former life."

"A former life, you say . . . yet, here we are," Edweene laughed quietly. "Fitting. The dead nun enters the grand Temple of Tears for the first time through the resting place of the dead."

"Fitting too," I said, "that I shall return to do The God's business through the passages where I was commanded to commit acts unspeakable in his name."

"We best be about it," she said. She waited till the guard was turned, then expertly, and silently slipped over the fence, and padded up behind him. At the last moment, he must have realized something was amiss, for he grunted loudly, "Oi!" and made to turn, spear in hand. But, it was too late, a quick knife to the throat, and she laid the man down at the foot of the door.

I followed her in, opening the gate and rushing up to her. The man stared into the sky, eyes open and mouth agape as if crying for God to take him home. I looked away from those eyes. I needed no more conviction for the murders I'd committed nor those of my allies. Silently, I signaled her, and we pulled him away from the door. I rested him against the wall to the side so as not to impede our progress, closed his eyes, and made the sign of the Star on my chest, beseeching The God for his forgiveness and allowance into his Kingdom.

"Hurry," she said, clearly annoyed by my reverence.

I nodded and went to the door. It took me a moment, but I soon found the secret latch that would open the door and pressed it. The stone slid and swung outward, revealing a blackened hole in the Mount. A stale smell wafted out, and shafts of the waning sun slipped inside, revealing a carved stone floor flanked by the corridor's stone walls inlaid with the words of The God's Canon inscribed at eye level, in meaningful passages every two or three paces.

"After you, my umbral lady," I murmured dryly. "Your tomb awaits."

"Ever the gentleman," Edweene sighed as she slipped past me, one hand trailing along the stonework as a guide.

I snatched the small lantern the guard had hung next to the door and followed. Despite my professed bravado, my nerves were on edge. Descending into that shadowed place felt like stepping over the precipice into a damned past that I'd left behind.

We soon passed the outer chambers, where the resting places of important Vestals had been cut into the walls, their corpses covered with holy vestments that hid their rotting remains from the eyes of passersby, and soon, we passed a larger set of passages, leading to the right and left, where the tombs of knights by the score were laid in the same manner. But vestments and shrouds did not cover them. Instead, they lay in armor and shield, their tunics rotting and falling to nothing, revealing the rusted mail beneath.

"Only a bit further," I whispered to the Lych, who proceeded like a cat ahead of me. "The priests shall be next, and there we shall find the way."

Though quiet, my voice echoed through the corridor. The lantern light cast her creeping shadow as a flittering demon on the path ahead. I shivered at the sight of it—such a haunting form for this frightening, beautiful woman. I thought to close my eyes and push the vision away when she said. "There, ser, ahead."

The priest's tombs—or should I say the tombs of the vicars and sextons that administered the Temple—rose from the darkness around us. More ornate than the knights or vestals, they were stone sarcophagi, inscribed with the words of The God. Three or four deep and a dozen long these tombs led us further on. Two more passages extended to the left and right, holding more of the dead. I remembered this place well, a dissonant, if hallowed place where the holiest of the holy received glorious burial, and, unbeknownst to them, provided the Temple's killers with free egress.

I pushed through, passing beside Edweene. Ahead, the ornate tombs of the Bishops of Tears rose from the darkness. Carved deep into the rock of the underworld, the crypts were adorned with intricate marble and silver details. The names of six bishops, representing a century and a half of authority, were immortalized in stone and flowing silver. *We all come to nothing,* I thought as I reached the end of the hall.

A great wall rose in front of us, my light glittering off the silver and gold inlaid letters of the Canon, the Verse of Eternal life. I read it aloud by force of habit, as I made the sign of the Star, on my chest:

For as The God was broken and entombed, so too did His divine spark flicker within the darkness. When agony and betrayal's bitter dregs ran coldest, and all hope lay spent, that eternal flame rekindled with the morn. Death's shroud was cast aside, and glory resurrected anew through faith's resilience and love's indomitable power. For only by descending into deepest shadow and drinking fullest of suffering's cup can the brightening path to forevermore be illumined and scaled by the righteous and the just.

The words stuck in my throat as I spoke them. I swallowed my fear and loathing at all that I was and what I had become. It was time to repair those things. This was no time for cowardice. We needed to reach the Earless before the end came.

Praying for deliverance, I handed Edweene the lamp. "Hold this, please. I need both hands for what is coming." I took a deep breath and steeled myself. Something felt ungodly here, like I was violating some sacred oath. *How has my Crusade come to this?*

She took the lamp and gave me a confident smile. "You are a good knight, Aaron. Remember this. All of this . . ." she symbolically waived the light around the room as if to show the dark grandeur around us, ". . . is for you. Not for the likes of Transom and Tooleb. The God is in you. She pressed her hand against my breast. I felt it's reassuring strength, and I breathed deeply. "He may not be here for me anymore. He may have left me, but he knows you, Aaron. You are his holy warrior if one exists. It is you."

I looked into those glittering blue eyes and nodded. I wanted to say, *The God has not abandoned you, Edweene. He never abandons those who have sacrificed like you.* But I remained silent. Now was not the time.

I turned and placed my hands on the opposing ends of the Star. And pressed with all the strength I could muster while whispering the written words of Eternal Life. The wall shifted, groaned, and slid backward. When it offset the wall, I leaned heavily on my left hand, and the great stone door swung inward. With a reverberating grinding sound, loud enough to wake entire legions of the dead.

Expecting to continue onward into the temple, I had not prepared to face my enemy yet, and was confused when three knights wearing the bishop's colors turned to face me. They sat at a table, drinking from tankards of mead, and playing Bones. They'd set their weapons on the

table among their belongings, various steel im-
plements of torture, and half-eaten plates of
food. Behind them, the Earless Monae, wearing
only her underthings and covered in the grime
of captivity, was strapped to a rough-hewn chair.
She remained unmoving, her head lolling on her
chest. Her breast rose and fell in shallow breaths.
Behind her, an arched passageway led away.

By the surprised looks on their faces, the three
huscarls clearly were unaware of the secret en-
tryway. Edweene, however, did not hesitate in the
slightest. She rushed past me in a flash, her thin,
curved saber flashing and taking the first one
under the chin. He fell over, his throat slashed to
the spine. The second knight was already moving, snatching his flail from the table and swinging it at Edweene, who deftly dodged out of its
way. I drew my sword and slipped up beside Edweene, deflecting the spear of the third, who had
stumbled backward, but lashed out with his long
spear over the top of the table.

After the first round, two Tears faced us. One
stood, his feet shoulder-width apart, reading
his flail. The second man was slightly back, his

spearhead held ahead of him, meant to keep us at a distance.

"So . . . you've come for the traitor," the spear-man said. "Don't know how you came here, but you shall die here, below the temple. We'll not allow you to defile the Holy Place."

"It has already been defiled, coward!" I spat back at him. "Torturing a woman is no knightly business—"

He charged me before I could finish my insult, his spear coming in fast and low. I made to deflect it away by bringing my sword forward against its length and turning it. But the spear-man was a competent fighter, had predicted my parry, and easily spun it up and back to the thrust. I danced backward just in time to avoid the point.

He grinned at me as his companion came on hard, swinging a large overhand attack at Edweene. She avoided the knight's attack by quickly sidestepping as the flail smashed through the table. She deftly launched herself forward and drove her saber into his open side. He stumbled back, dropped his weapon, and collapsed atop the Earless, who snapped awake. Seeing her exposed in making her thrust, the spearman tried to rotate and take advantage of the opening, but I was prepared. As he adjusted and brought his weapon around, I was on him, bringing my sword down on his forward hand and lopping it from his arm.

The man screamed, released his spear, took one last look at us, and fled through the back passageway, gripping his severed wrist.

"He is mine, tend to the Lady Monae," Edweene shouted and rushed after him, disappearing into the tunnel.

CHAPTER 13
A LYCH'S FORGIVENESS

The ropes binding the Earless fell away with each frantic tug of my dagger. I pulled her upright in the crude chair, cradling her face in my hands as her eyes fluttered open. Though marred by grime and the shadow of recent torments, I was relieved to see her proud spirit still burned defiantly.

"Easy, my lady," I murmured. "We have you, now."

Her brow furrowed as sharpened awareness crept back into her features. "Ser . . Aaron? But . . . how did you . . ."

A cry of alarm echoed from the adjoining tunnel where Edweene had given pursuit. The Earless immediately stiffened, her eyes widened with panic.

"Aaron, you must listen," she said, her voice raspy and intense. "The bishop's treacheries run deeper than you know. Tonight, during the royal audience, he means to murder the king himself!"

I went momentarily, dumb, I don't mind saying. The words hung there, leaden in the fetid air. The assassination of the King. We'd known it was coming, and soon. But, tonight we thought it would be simply the accusations against the Earless, and her allies. Of course—it made sense. It was the only way a conspiracy of this magnitude could truly grip the kingdom by its unholy throats. My mind raced. How long until . . . ?

"The crescent moon. Is it . . . ?" I whispered, and she nodded. "My lady, this takes place tonight?" I asked again, rhetorically, as though repeating it out loud would make it more real. I fought to keep the tremor of dread from my voice.

"It convenes within the hour," I said.

The Earless grimaced as she gingerly rose to stand. "I had lost track of time in this pit. By The God, Aaron, you must go at once. Stop this. Stop him."

The urgency in her eyes bore straight into my soul. I could not help but be impressed by the audacity of this woman's zeal for our king after receiving such torturous attention from our enemies. It humbled me to the core. I nodded, squaring my shoulders to the task.

"Then let's quit these shadows," I said grimly. "My companion and . . ."

My words trailed off as the sound of armored boots and clashing steel echoed closer from the corridor. With a harsh shove, I pushed the Earless behind me, snatching up my sword from the table where I'd set it. The silhouette of a large shape hurtled through the gloom and into the room, collapsing at my feet—a dead knight in the colors of the Bishop of Tears. Edweene followed, slamming into the wall beside me. She clutched her side as blood seeped through her fingers. She leaned on her curved blade to steady herself.

"Aaron . . . there are too many . . ." she wheezed, those preternatural eyes seemed to flicker with equal parts pain and rage and determination. I wanted to reach out and comfort her, see how bad her wound was, but her voice would brook no delay, "We must go . . . now, ser!"

The tortuous ringing of steel on steel grew deafening as two knights appeared in pursuit, hackles raised for blood. These were not Knights of Tears, but the bishop's own. Their blades glinted in the lantern light; their expressions twisted into snarling rictus in their open-faced helms.

There would be no quarter given here. No shred of decency to stay their merciless charge. To them, we were heretics and traitors who dared violate their precious temple.

"Take her out," I called to Edweene. "On the other side, there is a way to wedge the door. I hazard to say they don't know how to find the lever."

Edweene moved and grunted under the weight as she helped Lady Monae to her feet. She nodded to me grimly. "Hurry Aaron. And—"

I did not wait for her admonition to be safe. That was not in the dealing tonight. I was already charging to meet them, sounding a defiant roar.

They were expecting Edweene to continue her flight, and we're not expecting to see me at all, I think. My rush clearly surprised them, for their looks changed from rage and triumph to shock as I crashed into one, leading with my shoulder and following up with my knee to his cod. The man fell back into the corridor behind, skidding several feet and dropping his sword. His friend twisted to the side and brought his sword down toward me at an awkward angle. But, I was in too close, and, dropping my own sword, wrapped my arms around him and crushed him into the door jamb, knocking the wind out of him.

That second seemed a confluence of held breath and hammering fists as I pummeled his torso relentlessly. Then, with a guttural cry, I slipped my dagger fluidly from its belt sheath and slid it upward, under his chin, and into his head with a finessed, if violent, jab. I ripped it free, spattering in a wash of scarlet as it crumpled away, gasping at his last.

His fellow stood back now, balking and eying his sword on the ground—he faltered in open shock at my onslaught. But the energies coursing through me paid no heed. I was already slipping into another violent attack, shuffling forward aggressively as I snatched my own sword from the ground. I'd not let these men keep Edweene and the Earless from escaping if I could manage it. Whatever profane rapture she had unlocked within my battered soul, it had to be enough to get us from this place. It had to be.

The mailed forms of more Tears surged into view, farther down the hall. The singular opponent looked to be gaining courage from their presence as he edged forward toward me. Panic flared white-hot—we would run down if we did not get beyond that crypt door . . . and soon.

Gathering what shredded reserves I could muster, I readied to make one final, suicidal plunge toward them . . . when Edweene's voice called to me.

"Aaron! Now is the time. Come to me!"

I chanced a look behind; she and the Earless had opened the secret door and were beckoning me to follow. I turned, and feinted toward my cowed enemy, and he took a step back, dragged out his dagger . . .

But I'd already turned and fled through the door. I pressed my hands into the mechanism and activated the lock. The door churned and groaned and slid shut once again.

"Let's go, before they figure this thing out," she said. The Earless looked at the dark, shadowed tunnel, with all its corpses and tombs and breathed a deep sigh.

"What is this place?" she asked.

But I was already moving ahead. "Follow me," I said. More to her than to Edweene, who was already beginning our retreat through the way we'd come.

We pressed on, listening to the echo of their weapons and tools banging on the secret door. It was disconcerting, to say the least. But when it went quiet, it became even more so. My heart pounded and I held my breath as we rushed as quickly as Edweene could carry the wounded Lady Monae.

"Hurry," I exclaimed to bolster myself, and it echoed down the passageway like an angry warning from The God.

The echoes of steel shod boots and shouts of dismay and anger followed us down the haunting corridor. As we ran, the hallway behind us fell to blackness. But I glimpsed the orange of torchlight far behind. They'd found a way through. And they were coming on rapidly. I knew the lady was hurt, so I chose not to urge her any faster with useless words. I stopped, sheathed my sword, and wrapped her arm around my shoulder, then ushered us along faster.

Edweene dropped away from underneath her and drew her sword. "I'll watch the rear, Aaron," she said.

I acknowledged with a grunt and pushed ahead, nearly dragging my charge. Edweene placed her hand in my back, as much to keep contact as to push us ahead, as she watched behind. But I felt her urgency there, and it gave me resolve. I sped up, despite the lady's grunts and curses. But, despite it all, I could hear them closing on us, their strides long and rapid. They pursued with haste, running after us. Their voices came closer and closer as we fled.

Finally, I saw ahead of us the cracks of the tomb opening that would lead us into the Temple district.

"They are on us, Aaron. It was a valiant effort. Draw your weapon, and let us meet them," she called out. The hand left my back and I felt an immediate loss.

I cried out, "Don't give up, we are almost—"

The clang of steel on iron echoed violently down the remaining length of the corridor. I would not see her die alone. I slid the Earless off my shoulder and pointed toward the cracks. "Just there. We will hold them here. Get to the palace. Tell the king."

The terrified look in her eye was overshadowed by the determination in her voice. "he'll know your courage, Aaron—"

I turned and joined Edweene among the rush of Tears, her voice disappearing in the clang of my sword against a knight's skillful parry. A dozen or more had pushed up behind the lead two knights in the tunnel, helmets so deep, I could not see the end of them in the darkness. I ignored a sudden premonition of death and pressed ahead, pushing my opponent back amongst the corpses of a hundred long-dead nuns and vestals. He grinned at me and took a jab, which I deftly knocked away. I wondered if the Tears would add another Nun to the corpses here this night. Not if I had my druthers, I swore, as I danced away from another attack, and came shoulder to shoulder with Edweene.

"Like old times," I laughed darkly.

"Just like," she agreed, grunting as she stepped forward inside a knight's guard. He parried her sword away and came back at her. She dodged back, avoided his counter, and came up in high-guard position.

"We die here, Aaron. There are too many—"

A thunderous crash resounded from the chamber's entrance behind me. I spun around, and the lych instinctively filled the void so my back was not exposed. I raised my sword in the defense to this new threat, only to find the towering, steel-clad visage of Knight Commander Gavreaux striding forward. His visor was open, face set, and his blade and shield held at the ready.

"Passage Knights!" His voice was a stentorian bellow that echoed off the ancient stonework like an earthquake. "To me and the Lady Monae!"

The corridor erupted with the ring of steel on steel, and the hoarse shouts of men pushed suddenly into a crucible of combat once more. Human shapes materialized from the darkness—Crusader knights and sergeants loyal to my banner led by Ser Willem. They crashed into the Tears like a whirlwind, swarming past me and pushing me aside.

My knees nearly gave out, such was my relief. But Edweene was consumed with her abominable need. She waded into our enemies, slipping her saber into one's belly. Edweene's enemy fell away, dead, but two more filled his spot, swarming around her. There were still too many, even for the newly arrived knights. We were, after all in their lair. I tried to push forward, but found my way stemmed by another Tear. I parried his axe, and he deflected my counter, as Gavreaux himself rushed to Edweene's side.

I watched numbly as Gavreaux came up next to her and cleaved one of her opponents through the neck. He pushed another back with his kite shield. "Stay strong, my lady," he called. "You have done good work!"

She looked at him, her eyes wild, glittering blue as brilliant as blue flame. She said, conviction burning in each word, "I would kill all these bastards!"

But he pulled on her arm. "You will doom us all, my lady. I will die here with you, if you wish. But so too will Ser Aaron, and that would ruin the king."

The Lych's glassy eyes bore back into his as she pressed her shoulder to his shield arm. In a fraction of a moment, a silent communication seemed to pass between them—a weighty exchange of promises and purpose. I expected her to strike him, so filled with hatred she'd been for so long. But she only nodded as she deflected a deadly spear thrust. Then Gavreaux nodded too, and they began to work their way back toward our escape.

"Knights of the Passage!" he bellowed, sword poised high and proud before him. "To my side—let none of these traitorous dogs impede The God's work this day. The soul of this kingdom hinges upon your steel!"

With a ringing chorus of war cries, the knights reformed into a bristling semi-circle formation around us. In its impregnable heart, I pulled the Earless close—blood-spattered yet defiant, her focus was solely ahead as Gavreaux held the rear as we left the tomb.

We forced closed the tomb's doorway and wedged a sword between it and the ground so it could not be opened easily. We did our best to reinforce the make-shift lock. As we did so, Willem sidled up to me. "Always causing trouble, ser?" he said.

"Thank The God, you came when you did," I said and threw my arms around him.

"Do not thank me. Thank your sister. It is only by luck that Gavreaux was with me when she told me of your foolish plan, and knew of this entrance. Otherwise, I wager you'd be dead."

"Ha. Probably so, my friend. Regardless, I am grateful. But, now, we have to get to the audience chamber," I said as the pounding on the door intensified. "If the Bishop's murder stroke comes anywhere close to success . . ."

"Enough said," he intoned. Gavreaux had already formed up the Passage Knights and Crusaders. Knights, sergeants and soldiers fanned out around us in a ring of steel, forming a defensive perimeter as we caught our bearings. I clutched the Earless by her shoulders, staring intently into her eyes.

She placed a grimy palm against my cheek, silencing me with a resolute nod. "You simply must not let him perish, Aaron," she said fiercely. "No matter the costs."

I swallowed hard, the true gravity of our plight striking home. If we failed to stop this regicide, would the Kingdom itself survive the aftermath? My certainties, convictions—all would be rendered meaningless, and the Will of The God would be lost to the ages in the filthy ambitions of powerful men.

I steeled myself once more and nodded in return. "No matter the costs," I echoed, unsheathing my blade once more. To the King, to the Crusade, to all that we had sacrificed to reach this precipice.

"Passage Knights! Men of Rivershire!" I roared over the swelling din. "We head for the palace!"

A ragged cheer swelled from two score voices, Gavreaux raising his sword in affirmation. "We must go now, ser," he said. "The Tears will come around the flank, through Circle Road, soon, and we'd best be gone, not trapped against the Mount."

Edweene took me by the arm, looking up at me, intense blue eyes boring into mine.

She said, "It is time to end this, Aaron."

CHAPTER 14

ZEALOTS AND TRAITORS

We'd been moving quickly and had arrived in the palace before the Tears had, either by luck or by design—I was not entirely sure which. Gavreaux and I entered the palace and left the Passage Knights and Ser Willem's crusaders outside in the outer bailey. The palace guards would not allow such a force inside the inner courtyard. After a quick negotiation with the guards at the gate to the inner bailey and then again at the palace, Ser Gavreaux, myself, and Ladies Monae and Kira were inside the palace grounds.

"We'd best hurry," I said to Gavreaux, nearly out of breath. The man was indomitable. He strode with the purpose of a man who was used to leading in every situation. He nodded, chin set, eyes narrowed. "We certainly do," he answered back.

"Ladies," he said to the Earless and Kira. "Find your way to your apartments and keep your heads down and the doors locked. No warrant has been issued for you yet, but I fear it will come soon—if what you say is true, my lady. And I would have you well hidden. I think they will not likely look for you in the most obvious of places."

Kira shrugged. "My lord, she said, we may go to my apartment. The king's guard had already driven us out. I doubt they'd expect us to go back there. It would be counterintuitive, to say the least. There, I can find the lady a proper gown to don, if she would have a common Thayne's silks."

Landy Monae laughed, a sound I was not accustomed to hearing from the stoic woman. It was lyrical and sweet. "I suppose it is superior to my underthings and this robe the good Knight Commander could find for me. Your dresses would be welcome. I wish I felt safe in my apartment. I would send word to my garrison in the camps."

"No time, my lady," I said, but already Gavreaux was heading for the central palace. I left Kira with a cock of my head and a quick leave-taking bow, and I hurried to catch the commander. Once out of the residences, we found an abundance of nobles and their retainers heading toward the audience. We did our best to fit in, but our weapons, armor, mud, and blood-stained surcoats made us obvious to anyone, taking more than a passing glance.

None of that seemed to bother the single-minded Gavreaux. "Ser," I implored. "Should we be more discrete?"

"Ser," he said, in that dry way he had, "you spent too much time in skullduggery and subterfuge. Now is the time for direct action. The king is in danger."

"Yes," my lord. I followed in tow, feeling more like a child following his father than a knight on a mission to save the king.

In short order, we arrived in the ornate cause-way outside the large doors that would open into the great hall. The doors opened wide to accommodate the flow of nobles and courtiers into the hall. How word had spread about the importance of the audience was beyond me. How anyone knew it would be more than the weekly address to the court was a mystery for a different time. But clearly, the word had spread throughout the holy city. Everyone of note seemed to pack into the place—more witnesses for this abominable murder, I presumed.

"Where is the king?" Gavreaux asked the footman as we peered into the busy hall.

It was a massive place—the largest meeting place in the Holy Land, where the King and even the archbishop held court. Four rows of long tables—separated by a checkerboard floor, ran lengthwise to the front of the chamber, where the king's table headed up the back of the room.

The king's chair was positioned at center of the table, ornate in purples and reds, and rimmed in silver. Flanking the king were Bishop Tooleb's seat, along Gavreaux's, Transom's and Maester

Aldric's, and other of the high nobility of the Crusader cities. None of the king's entourage were seated yet. For a second, I wondered if they might use poison, but in this drama being orchestrated by the bishop, I doubted it. Steel would take the king tonight, or something even more debased, something that would make the earless a monster to all those within.

The guard shuffled sideways to give himself some distance from the throng. He eyed me with suspicion. "My lord, I think you should leave the palace. You don't want to be here. The bishop has made it known—though the whispers and innuendo—he will issue your warrant with the Earless'. It is a secret, but an open one—"

The knight commander interrupted him, saying, "Do not ignore my question, and if no warrant is issued, remain silent." Address me, man. I am—"

The great oak doors on the far side rumbled open, beckoning in a crush of finely dressed lords and ladies. Ornate tapestries depicting the glory of The God's divine journey adorned the vaulted ceilings far above, waved in the breeze caused released by the swinging door, and the causeway that led toward a balcony overlooking the Sea of Sorrows beyond. Yet the opulent grandeur of those tapestries and the sound of the distant sea seemed subdued against the cacophony of excited murmurs and not-so-discreet whispers filling the throne room's expansive chamber. It would not be long now before his Majesty entered the room.

"This way," Gavreaux muttered under his breath, guiding me through a discreet side entrance used by members of the royal court. Mere steps from the expectant throngs, a shadowed alcove opened into an interior hallway flanked by the customary posting of scarlet-clad Palace Guards.

Their captains snapped to dismayed attention at our grim, bloodstained appearances. "Ser Gavreaux—what is the meaning of this?" one demanded in a harsh whisper. His Grace is about to convene the audience." Recognition seemed to dawn on him, and his face went flat. "You, ser . . ." he pointed directly at me, ". . . You should not be here!"

"Silence, Captain," Gavreaux growled, daring the man to challenge us further, unimpressed impatience writ across his features. "There will be an attempt on His Majesty's life. We will not suffer any delays."

Stunned mutters rippled through the two soldiers until an ominous shadow fell over us. I turned with trepidation to find Transom bearing down on us. His pitiless, bone-carved face seemed to suddenly reflect every sin I'd endured, every horror and heresy the bishop meant to call down on the Crusade.

"Speak plainly, Brother Gavreaux," the Knight Commander intoned like a Temple judgement.

Gavreaux went rigid, lips peeling back from his teeth in a snarl of pure outrage. "Hold your tongue, charlatan! This very night, you and your rabid cult of maniacs are plotting to spill royal blood on these hallowed stones!"

A deathly hush fell over the hallway. The guards froze, caught between shocked horror and paralytic indecision. Transom slowly shook his head, features unreadable behind his dark eyes.

"Your slanders precede you, Brother. It is an ugliness I'll not further countenance. Disperse yourself and these brigands immediately, lest you face the Temple's imminent wrath."

As the two Knight Commanders closed into lethal range, a tremendous fanfare of trumpets pealed from within. The audience was beginning.

"Make way," a familiar rasp sounded behind me. "The reckoning you've sown comes to bitter fruit this eve . . ."

I whirled just as the shape of Ser Prenot hove into view. His face drew up, grim and nasty, in a dark smile, and he was clad in the bloody surcoat he'd worn in the hospital last night. Yet he held his sword steadfastly in front of him, the naked blade's edge glinting balefully in the torchlight.

"Prenot?" I gasped, recoiling in shock. "What madness grips you, boy?"

He laughed then—a thin, delirious sound that spoke of an unhingement of spirit utterly at odds with the friendly warmth that had once shone behind those eyes.

"This isn't just madness, Ser Aaron—it is revelation! Can you not see the Bishop's revelation laid plain all around us? His will is that of the Old Gods made manifest - the hour of their dominion and our salvation is finally at hand!"

With those last, unhinged words ringing in the ensuing silence, Prenot whirled and lurched towards the open doors. Down the center aisle the regal, backlit forms of the King and his privy council assembling ranks in stately, oblivious formation. The Bishop Tooleb stood at the King's side, staffed hand upraised in unctuous benediction as a throaty, tenor began to issue forth . .
.

"For too long, this kingdom has endured—a canker embedded within The God's house."

I surged forward with a strangled shout, but Prenot had gained a frenetic burst of speed in his madness. Like a shard of distilled hatred manifested, he seemed to plunge towards the King's exposed figure with the inevitability of a killing stroke fate had long decreed. All around me, pandemonium erupted—guards raising spears and sounding alarms, lords and ladies scattering in terror or frozen with uncomprehending horror.

But it all seemed so useless now that it came to it. I could not reach him in time . . .

Just as Prenot's sword made to pierce the man's breast, I sensed desperate movement flitting in the rafters above the seaside causeway under which the king and his retinue stood. Something lithe and impossibly rapid weaved from the shadows and fell between Prenot's blade and the doomed king.

And the clang of steel rang in the night as she drove his sword wide and drove in to trip him into a rolling fall. She gripped her side in pain as she came up to face him. But he had no time for her, found his footing, and launched himself past her toward the king.

In a whiplash of choked silence, the lych flung her off-hand forward, and gray smoking tendrils seemed to flow from her fingers to envelop his ankles in serpentine coils. Prenot fell and rolled, and cried out, "Witch, demon!" And came up after the king again, those abominable tentacles disappearing into the evening darkness as she fell down, holding her abdomen and groaning in abject pain.

But I was on him now, my sword knocking his weapon away and sending it spinning across the floor. The King's attendees turned and fled from the king, and the king stood firm, reaching for his own dagger, as the deranged Prenot struggled to regain his momentum.

I scrambled frantically to reach ahead and flung myself against Prenot in a bone-shattering collision. We slammed together in a tangled melee of flashing steel and choking grunts.

All sanity fled in those apocalyptic instants. Prenot became an impersonal killing monstrosity, hell-bent on our monarch's undoing, and I, a madman's berserker with only one purpose left: save the king, save the holy land.

"Demoness! Heretic Fiend!"

Maester Aldric's shrieking imprecation cut through the surrounding chaos as I gained the upper-hand and pinned Prenot against the ground. He peered up at me, his eyes held friendship and kinship—and madness. Sweat covered his pale face, and his mouth pulled back in an insane smile that belied the warmth in those eyes. I'd been here before, I suddenly realized. I'd been here before, looking down on Edweene those long years ago . . . and, like a strange, haunted, revisiting of that night long ago, I whispered to myself, "I am cursed," and I drove my dagger into Prenot's heart, sending him into merciful silence.

"You think to stand in His exalted path, you cursed demon?" Aldric spat at Edweene and rushed her drained body. "To deny this kingdom the blood-washed rebirth it hungers for, sickening abomination?"

I leaped to my feet and flung myself forward to defend my exhausted companion, but there was no way to get there in time. He raised his dagger, and I knew I was once again too late. I beseeched The God for mercy, and—

Aldric pitched sideways. His head separated from his body and rolled onto the causeway at the king's feet. The maester fell to the floor on the crimson carpet, his blood spreading and soaking into the velvety covering . . .

Behind him, Knight Commander Transom stood, bloody sword in hand, looking down at his bloody work.

CHAPTER 15
A NEW DAWN

The throne room descended into chaos after Ser Transom beheaded Maester Aldric. Courtiers screamed and scattered, guards rushed to secure the perimeter, and I stood in stunned silence for a moment before instinct kicked in.

"Edweene!" I shouted, sheathing my sword and rushing to her side. She hunched over, clutching her wounded abdomen, blood seeping through her fingers.

"I'm alright," she groaned through gritted teeth, with that typical stoic look she carried. Those piercing blue eyes met mine with dark determination. "See to the King."

Gavreaux and the king's guard had made a defensive circle that was already forming around the stunned monarch. Bishop Tooleb, having ended his benediction in a bloody battle, now waited behind them all. The cleric's face was ashen, dark, and brooding. His eyes, ever watching, took in all the goings on. I could sense he was working on some plot.

"Your Majesty, are you unharmed?" Gavreaux's voice boomed over the din.

The King nodded shakily, allowing his guards to pull him inside the ring of steel. "I . . . I do not understand what is happening here."

"Treason, Your Grace," Transom declared, striding forward with a bloody sword in hand. "Malign forces sought to strike you down this night. It is provident that Ser Aaron and my counterpart, the Knight Commander from the Passage, were in attendance to root out this heresy." He gave me a cynical nod of his head.

My heart jumped into my throat. The man was usurping the moment. A moment that he had created for—

I barked out a bitter laugh at the man's audacity. "You mean the same 'malign forces' you were allied with until just now? You, ser are beyond reproach. We have only just come from—"

Transom whirled on me; his expression was twisted with fury. "Mind your tongue, ser! I have simply done what was required to preserve the Church and Crown from profane conspiracy."

"Aaron!"

I turned to the sound of Kira's voice. She rushed in, the Earless Monae at her side, her eyes wide with bewilderment as she took in the surrounding scene.

"What is this madness?" the Earless demanded. She took in the scene. Her son lay crumpled beneath me, my dagger in his chest. I cast her a sad, almost apologetic look, as my heart fell. His eyes were suddenly there again, in my mind, looking up at me as I destroyed yet another person. She rushed to him, a longing, desperate look on her face. I stepped away, not wanting to impede or infect this moment with my presence.

She collapsed on his body, embracing him, laying her head on his chest and hugging his corpse to her. "No. No . . . not both my sons . . ." she wailed and sobbed.

"I . . . am . . . " I could not find the words to convey my despair, my guilt at having taken him, no matter the cause. I'd saved him once, and I'd killed him now. I could not help thinking of another . . . I cast a baleful look toward Edweene, who was struggling to sit up, already her dark powers drawing on the darkness of the scene to weld together her broken body.

She gave me her, I'm sorry for you, look, her blue eyes holding more compassion than all the words in all the bishop's sermons. My head dropped. My shoulders drooped just a little as I fought to find meaning in all this.

"The scroll," she said. "Aaron . . . the scroll. Do not let your pain draw you from our purpose. More count on you than just me or the Earless."

Her voice drew me from my self-reflection . . . I pulled the sealed scroll case from where I had secured it at my belt, its ornate carvings glinting balefully in the torchlight. It was everything now. It held—I hoped—the evidence that would doom the conspirators. I hefted it for the assembled court to see and cried out loud above the din and chaos.

"This, Your Majesty, is the profane conspiracy of which the good Knight Commander speaks." I locked eyes with the pale faced Tooleb. "Would you care to explain its contents to those assembled, Bishop? Or shall I break the seal?"

Tooleb opened his mouth, but no words came out. The King's gaze bored into him, silently demanding answers.

"Do it," the Earless said, her voice thick with the sound of her broken heart, firm with conviction despite her despair. "Let the truth be known, ser! Let everyone know why my sons are dead."

Muttering a silent prayer, I made the sign of the Star on my chest. God had brought me here. I had been the tool of reform and cleansing; there was no doubt of that to me. I asked for a little more strength . . .

I cracked the wax seal and unrolled the scroll. From the corner of my eye, I could see the bishop edging forward, a zealot's expectation on his face, as though he relished this reckoning. Ser Transom shifted uncomfortably. My eyes scanned the elegant script, and my heart turned to lead in my chest. I scanned the room, rolling the implications over in my head.

And suddenly, Willem was there, leading the Passage Knights and our men through the main doors. The palace soldiers were forming inside the great hall, while the Tears had occupied the ground in force. The Hall was filling with steel, and men were on edge.

Kira padded up to me and slipped her hand around my waist. She saw the trepidation on my face. "There is nothing to be gained from fear, brother," she said. "All you have done has brought you here. All we have done has brought you here. You must trust in The God. This is His place."

I cast a last look to Edweene, who smiled a pain filled smile. I smiled back. And then, I read the cursed document, raising my voice to carry over the hushed stillness.

"Brother Transom,

The hour is finally upon us to enact the purifying flame of justice. We have labored long and hard for this day, when we will finally enact the purifying flame of justice upon this pretender who fails to use the Crusade as it should be used, and we will free the Holy Land from the shadow of the Old Gods and their dark minions, the Gol. Our assassin is a nobleman, with naught but loyalty to The God, has sworn to dispatch the king before as many witnesses that we can engineer. So, wait for the hall to be full. Wait for my benediction. We must be beyond reproach.

Ser Prenot shall meet you there in the morning. And my men, who keep the Earless under your Temple, shall bring his mother. The two together shall make a fitting sacrifice for The God. She, a dupe, and he, the holy warrior who will spark this war, as he almost did in the shadow of Caer Gorak. If only we could have sparked this war, without such drastic measures. The God works as The God works.

Only then can we let the crusaders' rage be unleashed upon Gol, and liberate this Holy Land forever. Once her to-conspirators' are slain in the act, and your coronation by the Council of Kings is complete, the Earless will be kept isolated in the cells until a public execution can be arranged.

Her death must become a cauterizing fire that burns away any lingering doubts as to our resolve and righteousness in these coming days of upheaval. An example made to show any who would deal with the enemy within that no quarter shall be given.

Stand vigilant, brother. God's judgment is not far now. Soon the flames of rebirth will scour this sinful kingdom clean, and from those ashes shall rise a new order embracing the ascendant truth of the The God, and the Path of the Star.

--For His Tears, we do this, His Excellency, Bishop Tooleb"

As the words of the accursed document rang out, I saw the blood drain from Transom's face. The Knight Commander staggered back, shaking his head in denial even as the stark realization crept in. He had taken a gamble and failed, a pawn in Tooleb's unholy game.

When the bitter truth was spoken in full, a profound silence hung over the audience chamber, and the Knights of Tears, almost as one, stepped back into the shadows of the room as if to acknowledge their humiliation at their leader's complicity. I assured myself that there would be redemption there over time, for these knights who had served God so faithfully for so long and now struggled with this scar tissue and shame. All other eyes turned towards the disgraced bishop, awaiting his response.

But Tooleb proved to be more resilient than I expected. Lifting his chin defiantly, he spat, "Blasphemous lies! This is a pathetic forgery, no doubt concocted by that profane thing."

He pointed a crimson finger at where Edweene kneeled, glaring hatefully. In a flash, Gavreaux crossed the open causeway, and his blade was at the bishop's throat, his eyes burning with righteous fury.

"That 'thing', as you so crudely put it, saved your king's life this night, you miserable wretch," the Knight Commander snarled. "I would now hear her words over your serpent's tongue any day."

"He's right," a soft voice rang out. All eyes turned towards the source—the frail, bloodied form of the Earless Monae. Despite her battered state, she stood tall and unbowed, pinning Tooleb with her diamond-hard glare.

"I can attest to the legitimacy of that scroll, Your Grace," she declared. "For I was imprisoned beneath the Temple of Tears on the bishop's orders, accused of treason against the Crown through forgeries of his own making. I was beaten, and ... defiled ..."

The King looked from the Earless to the defiant Tooleb, and a muscle twitched in his weathered jaw.

"Guards," he said, at last, his voice tight but steady. "Take the Bishop of Tears and the Knight Commander into custody to await judgment for their crimes." He turned to one of his attendants and beseeched him to act, saying, "Send word to the archbishop. I have no authority to pass judgment on his cleric." See that he receives none of the courtesies his station once afforded."

As the scarlet-liveried guards moved to carry out his order, I expected Tooleb to shatter, to rage and bluster at this reversal of fortune. Instead, a sly grin spread across the bishop's lips, his eyes glinting with something akin to ... satisfaction?

"You think you've won, child?" he hissed at the King. "That by removing me from the equation, all will be put, right? No . . . this is merely a temporary delay. The God knows what must be done. You'll see. You'll all see!"

With those cryptic, maddened words hanging in the air, the guards hustled the disgraced bishop from the chamber. An uneasy silence fell over those remaining, heavy with unspoken questions and troubling portents of what might yet lay ahead.

In the end, it fell to Gavreaux's level baritone to cut through the tension. Sheathing his blade with a dry rasp of steel, the grizzled knight met my gaze.

"Well struck, Ser Aaron. Your perseverance has saved us all from calamity this day."

I managed a grim nod of acknowledgment, feeling suddenly and profoundly weary down to my very bones. Nearby, Edweene had risen to her feet, leaning heavily on Kira for support. She offered me a small, enigmatic smile—a look I knew all too well after our long road together. Our eyes met, and some unspoken understanding seemed to pass between us.

"Ser Aaron, you have proven yourself this day, again, despite our prejudice against you."

"I follow . . . I try to follow the will of The God, Majesty," I said. "It is not often easy."

The King regarded me thoughtfully, then nodded as if he had already surmised the root of my inner conflict. "I suspected as much. Your path is your own to walk, Ser Aaron. May you find the peace you seek, for you have earned it a hundredfold."

With a final sweeping look over the crowd, the King turned and allowed his attending nobles to shepherd him from the chamber, no doubt to begin sorting out the fallout of this night's tumultuous events. The rest of the assembly quickly followed in their wake, until only a small, solemn cluster remained—myself, Edweene, Kira, the Earless Monae, and Gavreaux himself.

"Well," the gruff knight said at last with an amicable grunt. "It would seem we have all been rather put through the millstone on this most auspicious of evenings."

"So it would seem," I agreed, managing a weary smile.

Kira looked from me to Edweene and back, her expression a mixture of joy at our victory and melancholy at whatever lay ahead. The Earless simply watched in her usual inscrutable silence, still kneeling with her son, eyes swollen with tears.

"What will you do now, Aaron?" Kira asked, her voice hushed. "Where does your path lead from here?"

"I . . ." I began, then paused as the depth of the question's implications struck me fully. For so long, I had defined myself solely by the Crusade, by righting the wrongs done to the Holy Land. But in that moment, with the immediate threat addressed and the future unknown, I found my purpose less certain.

My gaze drifted towards Edweene, who regarded me with those haunting, depthless blues. There is so much still unspoken between us, so much potentially left to sacrifice if I choose to embrace the destiny before me.

"I'm not sure, little sister," I said at last. "But I suspect the first step lies in discovering what matters most . . ."

With that, I turned away, feeling several sets of eyes upon my back as I to where Edweene sat upon a bench, nursing an old wound. She looked up at me quizzically as I stopped before her.

"Well?" she asked, a hint of her usual sharpness undercutting the simple word.

I pulled in a deep, steadying breath. "We should discuss matters."

Edweene's eyebrow quirked upwards, but she said nothing as she pushed herself up from the wall and joined me, leaving the others to their solemn victory celebrations.

*

Weeks passed in the wake of that fateful night. The Holy City slowly returned to some semblance of normalcy, though the dark cloud of Tooleb's malign ambitions would forever stain its holy ground.

I stood alone on a balcony overlooking the Sea of Sorrows, watching the tireless tides roll endlessly against the rocky shores far below. A warm, coppery dawn was just cresting over the horizon, banishing the shadowed vestiges of night.

Soft footfalls sounded on the polished marble behind me, but I did not turn, already knowing who had come to join my solitary vigil.

"It's time," Edweene said, her voice tinged with an undercurrent of melancholy.

I closed my eyes, taking in the fresh ocean breeze and letting it wash over me like an ancient benediction. At long last, I had found the answer I had been seeking—or perhaps, it had found me.

"Yes," I murmured in reply. When I opened my eyes, Edweene stood at my side, her dark features uncharacteristically unguarded and vulnerable in the pale dawn's light. At that moment, it was almost possible to glimpse the young woman of faith who had once walked Pilgirm's Approach before tragedy and torment remade her into something darker . . . something transcendent.

"You're leaving, then?" she asked, averting her eyes as if unable to look upon me for too long. "Truly this time?"

I sighed and reached out, trailing my fingertips across the soft skin of her cheek. She started at the contact but did not pull away, watching me with those penetrating blue eyes.

"I must, Edweene," I said simply. "This ... what lies between us . . .whatever destiny has been shaping us towards all this time . . . I cannot embrace it fully until I've made atonement for past sins. Not yet."

Edweene leaned into my touch, and I felt as if my calloused palm was cradling some heartrendingly fragile thing that might shatter if handled too roughly.

"You seek The God's forgiveness?" she asked, a glimmer of hurt flickering in her eyes despite her attempts to mask it. "After all, we've endured . . . you still cling to that path?"

In answer, I reached up with my other hand and gently stroked her yellow hair, letting the silken strands flow between my fingers.

"The path has changed," I murmured, hardly daring to speak the tenderness aloud. "We have walked in shadow for far too long. I aim now to find the light at the journey's end . . . and pray you will one day feel its warmth as well."

A tremulous smile touched Edweene's lips at that, a lighter spark flaring briefly behind those mercurial depths. Without warning, she pulled me into a fierce embrace, resting her forehead against my chest as our hushed breaths mingled.

"Prayers are the beginnings of promise," she whispered, so close that I could feel the sultry tremor of her words like a shivery caress. "I have not prayed in a long time. I fear The God will not hear me. But, I shall not abandon hope while you seek such purity of purpose. I do, as you know, have eternity on my side."

And just like that, she was gone—a fleeting brush of silken fingers across my cheek, the only evidence she had been there at all. I blinked and turned, but the balcony was empty, the rising sun's aureate touch spreading across the polished stone in Edweene's wake.

Yes, the path ahead was still long and arduous, but I no longer walked it alone. Not truly. Turning back towards the Sea of Sorrows, I stood for a long moment and simply let the rhythmic tides fill my senses. When I finally turned and strode from the balcony, it was with a renewed sense of purpose and a lightness of spirit I had not felt for far too long.

A new dawn had broken over the Holy Land, after all. One that promised a chance for redemption . . . and perhaps something more.

Somewhere in the darkness, a raven cawed.